Praise for *Lunch at the Piccadilly*

"Edgerton's is one of the most graceful and humane studies of old age we could hope to find."
—*The Washington Post*

"As in all of Edgerton's fiction, themes of love and duty, family and friendship—this time examined in the context of growing old—transcend any boundaries of geography or gender."
—*The Atlanta Journal-Constitution*

"For sheer likability, it'd be hard to beat Edgerton's affectionate portraits of small-town oddballs in the South. His eighth outing is a breezy comedy, tinged with sadness. . . . Another small gem from Edgerton."
—*Kirkus Reviews*

"With wry humor and priceless dialogue, Edgerton pulls off the near-impossible—he turns a nursing home into the most convivial of establishments. . . . With equal parts skill and whimsy, Edgerton creates a screwball portrait of this 'life after life,' effortlessly convincing us that it's better, *much* better, to laugh than to cry about it."
—*ALA Booklist*

"The novel blends humor and sadness to a remarkable degree. Edgerton . . . is a treasure."
—*Library Journal*

"*Lunch at the Piccadilly* is a deceptively simple tale that brims with compassion and wisdom, weaving laugh-out-loud pieces with infinitely tender observations about the human condition. . . . Once again, Edgerton has crafted a little treasure of a novel—funny, wistful, packed with truth and humanity."
—*The Charlotte Observer*

Lunch at the Piccadilly

Lunch
at the
Piccadilly

a novel by

Clyde Edgerton

BALLANTINE BOOKS • NEW YORK

A Ballantine Book
Published by The Random House Publishing Group

Copyright © 2003 by Clyde Edgerton
Reader's Guide copyright © 2004 by Clyde Edgerton
and The Random House Publishing Group, a division
of Random House, Inc.

www.ballantinebooks.com/BRC
Book design: Anne Winslow

ISBN 0-345-47678-6

This edition published by arrangement with Algonquin Books of Chapel Hill.

Manufactured in the United States of America

9 8 7 6 5 4 3 2 1

First Ballantine Trade Paperback Edition: September 2004

For Louis Rubin

CONTENTS

Acknowledgments

With appreciation for advice, stories, and sketches from
Buddy Swain, Sharon Boyd, Jim Boyd, Cotton Tyler,
Jill McCorkle, Ola King, Paul and Betty Mushak, Emerson
McReynolds, Lila Spain, Buster Quin, Catherine Edgerton,
George Terrl, Louis Rubin, Doris Betts, Dan Glass, June
White, Mary Hood, David McGirt, Barbara Penick, Joe
Mann, Jack Stanley, Anita Loehr, Vic Miller, Jean Mincey,
Rachel Careau, Bill Kicklighter, the Warrens, the Haileys,
the Penicks, the Edgertons, and the Joneses.

Thanks to the creative writing faculty and students at
the University of North Carolina at Wilmington for their
inspiring creativity, to Richard Elliott Friedman, author
of *Who Wrote the Bible?*, and to Sallie Tisdale, author of
Harvest Moon.

And with special thanks and appreciation to my editor,
Shannon Ravenel, and my wife, Kristina.

Portions of this book appeared in significantly different
versions in *Novello: Ten Years of Great American Writing*,
Carolina Quarterly, *Descant*, *Witness*, *Image: A Journal of the
Arts and Religion*, and *The Raleigh News and Observer*.

Lunch at the Piccadilly

Prologue

❧

Q. (From you, gentle reader.) I'm just here to more or less see what the arrangements will be for my aunt. Like, how does Medicare work for somebody coming in here?

A. (From small woman with dyed-black frizzy hair, wearing large, thick 1970s glasses. She is sitting at the financial desk at your local nursing home.) First of all, I suppose you know about the hospital. Medicare will cover the first sixty days but not the first seven hundred and sixty-four dollars of a benefit period. A benefit period is up when the patient hasn't gotten any skilled care in a nursing home—like here at Rosehaven—for sixty days.

Q. Okay. Does that . . . she's qualified to be covered here, isn't she? For a certain period or something.

A. Oh, yes.

Q. So how does that work?

A. Well, now, Medicaid can pick up where Medicare leaves off, but you have to meet certain requirements that have a lot to do with hardship and giving out of money, but which Mr. Rhodes did not want to instigate here. Mr. Rhodes owns the place, so we don't really do

Medicaid. Medicaid could cover that first seven hundred and sixty-four dollars, for example. For the hospital stay.

Q. What about here? How does that work? Medicaid —I mean Medicare. I haven't had a chance to—

A. Well, the way it works here is that the coinsurance comes in on the twenty-first day, after twenty days, and Medicare covers everything through day one hundred above ninety-five dollars and fifty cents a day, which is what you have to cover. That used to be true for over sixty days in the hospital.

Q. What about those first twenty days?

A. Was she in a hospital for three days *in a row, not including her departure day*?

Q. Yes, she was there for four days.

A. And that was not over thirty days ago?

Q. No, she just got out.

A. Then all she needs is certification, which I'm sure she has.

Q. How much does Medicare cover, then, for those first twenty days?

A. Essentially everything. That's for twenty days. And if she leaves somewhere in there and wants to come back, she can't unless she's been in a hospital for three consecutive days, with her discharge day the day after the third day. See what I mean?

Part 1.

The First Breakfast

Older People in Cars

CARL TURNAGE TAKES SLOW, short steps so he won't get ahead of his aunt Lil. They move along toward her maroon 1989 Oldsmobile sitting in the shade. It's easy to spot because of the luggage rack on the trunk lid. They are headed to the Piccadilly for lunch, and after that he'll let her practice-drive in the mall parking lot. Carl has mixed feelings about the driving part. Today will probably be the last time his aunt will ever drive a car— and it's his job to break that news.

"Is that my car?" she asks. Humped over and thin, she holds to the arms of her walker. She wears gold slippers, tan slacks, Hawaiian shirt, striped jacket, and makeup that stops along her jaw like the border of a country.

"Yes ma'am. I washed it."

"Well, it looks good."

"I'll let you drive it a little bit after we eat."

He helps her into the passenger seat. Her head seems about as high as the button on the glove compartment. In her three months at Rosehaven Convalescence Center, she seems to have steadily shrunk—from osteoporosis—and has fallen twice but somehow not broken a bone. He folds her walker, and as he lays it in the backseat, her sunglasses drop out of her saddlebag and slide under the passenger seat. He retrieves them.

Back when Carl started driving, Aunt Lil owned a used 1968 Ford Mustang convertible, white with red interior. She let Carl drive it at least one Saturday night a month, as well as to his senior prom.

At the mall they park in their normal spot on top of the big two-deck parking lot.

In the cafeteria line, with tray rails to hold to, Aunt Lil doesn't need her walker. Carl folds it and takes it on his arm.

This is a long lunch break for Carl. He's a contractor at Richardson's Superior Awning and Tile, and sometimes, on simple, straightforward jobs, he leaves his second-in-command, Juan, in charge of the other four or five workers.

Aunt Lil chooses chicken chow mein without rice. He gets it with rice.

Carl's aunt Sarah, who died last year, once said that

stopping driving was the worst thing she'd ever been through, including (1) her husband's death, (2) her daughter's divorce—it was a bad one—and (3) watching her dog Skippy get run over. Aunt Sarah was the last living of all his aunts and uncles besides Aunt Lil. She was the one who said that if she'd known she was going to live as long as she did, she'd have bought a new mattress.

Aunt Lil told that story when she bought *her* new mattress. That was about a month before she fell in her tub, twice on the same night. She managed, after the second fall, to get out of the tub and call Carl on the phone, and that night was the beginning of her downward drift, her gradual failing of mind and body, a decline less abrupt than his mother's or Aunt Sarah's.

On Aunt Lil's tray is a plate of chow mein, a biscuit, a little dish of broccoli with cheese sauce, and iced tea. On Carl's, chow mein over rice, fried okra, string beans, fries, cucumber salad, pecan pie, and a Diet Coke. At the cash register, Aunt Lil reaches for his little white ticket slip and puts it with hers. She'll insist that he pay with her MasterCard.

A cafeteria worker carries Aunt Lil's tray to one of her two favorite tables. Aunt Lil and Carl sit, Carl says the blessing, and they begin eating. He is never quite sure if he should say the blessing when he's with her. Unlike his mother and Aunt Sarah, Aunt Lil has more or less given up on church. They don't talk about it. Carl figures that's one of the things they can talk about sometime, though now that they are the only two left—and now that he too has drifted away from the shore, as that old gospel song says.

He watches her look around for old friends. They talk about normal things. He checks his watch.

"Have you met Mr. Flowers?" she asks. "With that fancy white hair?" She pictures him, the new resident, rolling in his wheelchair out onto the porch—his leg stuck out straight ahead, a big smile on his reddish face. He's a dandy.

"The one with the knee operation?" asks Carl.

"Yes. The preacher."

"We talked a little bit the other day."

"Where did you see him?"

"On the porch. You were with me."

"On . . . ?" Why doesn't he speak up?

"On the *porch*. When you were smoking a cigarette. You know, if you'd let me take you up to the hearing-aid place, I think we could get you fixed up."

"I can hear okay. People's talking has just fell off some."

"I think it's your hearing that's fell off some."

Sometimes, she thinks, he's almost as bad as his mama used to be—pressing a point. "My hearing's fine." She takes a drink of tea. "Somebody said Mr. Flowers is a Baptist, and somebody else said a Pentecostal. He seems to have a little personality—I guess that means he's a Pentecostal."

"What do you mean?"

"You know how Baptists are."

"I know Baptists with personality."

"You know what I mean."

"What?"

Aunt Lil laughs. "I don't know exactly." She isn't sure how to talk to Carl about religion. His mama was so devout. Sarah too.

"Mama had personality," says Carl.

"You know what I mean. Sometimes they seem kind of dead. Baptists. I don't mean your mama, for goodness' sakes. And I'm sure there are some lively ones around. Well, I know there are." Now that Carl's mama has died, a kind of torch has been handed to her, Lil, though she'd never say that out loud. It's all connected to her wanting a child and never having had one. Now that only she and Carl are left, maybe she can tell him about that lost boy from Tad's former marriage, about how Tad tricked her, about how . . . but what good will it do to tell him all that? It's old stuff, over the dam, spilt milk. It doesn't matter.

Carl glances at his aunt's hand to see how steady it is. Within the last year, she's begun to shake noticeably. The Taylor sisters—his mother, Aunt Sarah, Aunt Lil—practically raised him, the only child among the three of them, and now that he is caring for the last living one, he carries a vague fear that he's on the brink of a great silence.

He can't quite name his fear, a fear somehow related to the coming loss, probably not too far away, of Aunt Lil, the last person of the generation before him—both sides of his family, aunts and uncles. And he can't decide *how* that fear is related, though he feels it is, to the fact that he's only five feet six and speaks in a relatively high voice. Up into his twenties, he'd been expecting to—had been told that he would—grow taller and speak more deeply, and he had always imagined that when that happened, he would be fully grown up. But it didn't happen. He stayed relatively short and high-voiced, and now here's Aunt Lil, perhaps in her last year or two, maybe three. When she dies, his family—all the main ones—will be gone, will be no more. And he's still not as tall and deep-voiced as he ought to be, had hoped to be.

But maybe—to make things easier when she does die —there'll be a little money to cushion the blow. His few distant cousins have moved away, he is Aunt Lil's favorite by far, and she is the only one of the three sisters with money in the bank at the end of her life. But then again, Rosehaven will quickly eat up whatever she has.

THE TOP DECK of the two-decker parking lot is about the size of a football field, with a couple of ramps leading down to the ground-level deck below it.

Carl drives—with Aunt Lil in the passenger seat—to the far end of the almost empty lot, away from the mall.

He stops, gets out, helps her out of the passenger side, gets the walker from the backseat, then follows along as she pushes it around the back of the car to the driver's door. He helps her in, opens the back door, folds her walker, and places it inside so nothing will slide out of the saddlebag. From the passenger seat, he hands her the key. She puts it in the ignition, turns it, starts the car right up— it idles fast—and looks around.

That is probably the last time she'll turn that key, he thinks.

"Where's the exit?" she says. She seems determined, almost angry.

"We're just going to drive around up here on top for a few minutes and let you get the feel of things."

"What?"

"We're just going to—the brake's already released— we're just going to drive around up here on top for a few minutes and let you get the feel of things."

"I got the feel of things." She trusts the memory in her hands and feet to do right. It's been a while, she thinks, but all this is the same as riding a bicycle. Once you get it, you've always got it. Carl shouldn't have waited so long to let her do this. But he was a good boy, all in all— never gave Margaret and Jacob any trouble. And now she doesn't know what she'd do without him. She'll show him she can drive as good as he can, as good as anybody can.

She pulls the gear thing into drive, and they're off—in a big circle. You just steer it, she thinks, and everything falls into place.

"Where's the exit?" She wants to get out on the highway. Get on with it.

"We're going to stay up here on top, Aunt Lil. You can drive over toward those other cars if you want to. Maybe a little slower."

"I want to drive back. I need to get out on the highway."

"No ma'am, just—"

"There's a exit!" She swings the car to the left, and whoops!—they're going down a ramp. And it's dark. Good gracious.

Carl strains to see straight ahead, right hand on the dash, left reaching to touch the hand brake. Thank goodness the ramp is straight down, not curved. He thinks about pulling up the hand brake but decides against it: she needs to see, to prove to herself, what she cannot do.

The front left tire scrapes the curb. The car stops.

"What's that?" asks Aunt Lil.

"We drifted left. Let's pull on straight ahead, on down there beside that column, and I'll take her back over." He'll let her drive down there by herself. And that will be it—the end.

She starts out slowly, drifts right, and runs against the curb again. "What's wrong?" she asks.

"You keep running up against the *curb*."

"Oh." She looks over at Carl. "Am I driving?"

"Yes, *yes*. You're driving. Pull straight down to the bottom and I'll take back over."

"I need a little more padding under me. I'm too low in this seat."

"I don't think that's the basic problem, Aunt Lil."

At the bottom, just off the ramp, she stops the car.

Carl takes a deep breath. This is the time to tell her, he thinks, but . . . "Okay. Put it in park."

He gets out, opens the back door on the passenger side, gets out her walker. He's sort of preparing his speech. He wants to make it as easy as possible on her, to kind of set it up so she might make the suggestion herself, set it up in such a way that if she doesn't take the bait, then he'll say, Aunt Lil, I think you're just going to have to give up driving. Simple and straightforward. And then he'll say something like, I'll be able to get good money for your car, and then you won't have to pay for all that insurance and repairs and all that.

As he passes around the back of the car, he sees her head leaning into the middle of the car, looking down at something. Then he notices one of her feet hanging out the open door. "Be sure it's in par—"

The car is . . . both gold slippers are now hanging out the door, her head is back up, her hands are on the steering wheel—and the car is moving away, like a ship leaving port, her door and the passenger door wide open.

He lifts his hand, opens his mouth.

The car is moving along in a wide circle at about two miles an hour, missing one of those big columns, then another, circling around. He glances down. He's standing in the damn walker.

Free at last, she's thinking. Thank God Almighty, I'm free at last. But where in the world did he go? What is he trying to do? Now she'll have to go back around and get him. She'll just drive on around in a big circle here. That would be easiest. She doesn't seem to need to do anything with her feet. There is no clutch in this one, is there? She clearly remembers her Ford Roadster. What a car! Boy, *that* one had a clutch! How about that time before she and Tad were married when they went to the state fair and she let Tad drive, and the man directing traffic wouldn't look at them, and Tad just ran the car up against him, so that he ended up sitting on the hood? And what about that time he almost drove it off the high rock at the old quarry? She's been through the mill with automobiles. That's for sure. And Carl sure loved that Mustang.

She'll steer clear of all those big columns and go back and get him, for goodness' sakes. But why are her feet outside? Well, there's no need to bring them back in, it looks like.

Carl watches, his mouth open. She seems to be steering. He decides just to stand and wait, because it looks like she might come on back around. Something tells him if he hollers, she'll try to get out.

Here she comes. He sees the front left headlight as the car turns toward him. Then there is the full front end. The car looks like it's smiling. Just over the steering wheel he sees the top of her head. Can she *see?* He sets the walker behind a column, takes a few steps so he'll be on the driver's side when she comes by. There are those gold slippers just under the open door. Now he can see her eyes above the steering wheel. Here she comes. Man, this is something. He starts walking beside the open door— breaks into a slow trot, puts his hand on the door. For a second he visualizes himself in the Secret Service.

"You need to put it in *park,*" he shouts. She's looking straight ahead, frozen.

Wham! An explosion—and pain. He has run into a column. He staggers backward and then heads out after the car. He runs to the passenger door, jumps in, grabs the hand brake between them, and pulls it up slowly and firmly.

"Where'd you go?" she asks.

"Where'd I go?"

"Yes."

"I didn't go anywhere." He touches his head. A bump is rising. He looks at his hand to see if there is any blood. No.

"Well," she says, "you just disappeared."

"You drove off without me, Aunt Lil."

"Why?"

"I . . . That's a good question. Here. Let me get the keys." He reaches over, cuts the engine, and pulls the keys from the ignition. He looks at her. Her back is to him. He feels sorry for her, decides they can talk after he gets her to Rosehaven and they're settled in her room and he has eaten a couple of Tootsie Rolls. She keeps Tootsie Rolls in her blue bowl for everybody who comes in. He buys them for her, along with bananas, apples, and sugar-free candy.

Through a Glass Eye Darkly

ON THE DRIVE BACK to Rosehaven, Carl thinks of Anna Guthrie, the social worker there. Maybe he can stop by her office and talk to her—about Aunt Lil and this driving business. She has experience with this sort of thing.

Anna, ten years or so younger than he, is exactly what—or who—or rather the kind of person he can see himself marrying, when he gets around to that, maybe before too long. He stops in and says a few words to her once in a while, words spoken with relaxed vocal cords, dropping the pitch of his voice a good bit—and the topic is always his aunt, of course. He never stays very long, because then he'd have to think up other things to talk about. That's one reason he's not married. He doesn't like to sit with another person through silences, and he also doesn't like to talk a lot. He pictures himself stopping in and saying to Anna, Let me ask you something: how do you tell them they can't drive anymore? And then he'd tell her the whole story about the afternoon, along with those funny things his aunt Sarah once said about giving up driving. That will make Anna laugh. She has a good laugh.

She also has photographs on her desk of two little girls. But she doesn't wear a wedding ring. The girls may be her nieces.

Marriage. The whole business of it. He's not altogether sure he can make somebody happy. His mother and aunts and uncles hadn't seemed all that happy in marriage, something he dimly felt—but never thought about—while growing up. He'd felt a sadness hovering around Aunt Lil and Uncle Tad's marriage but never asked her about any of that.

And there's something else, a simple secret. He doesn't like the thought of undressing in front of a woman; but on the other hand, he knows he's okay sexually—he had enough experiences during his stint in the navy to prove that.

That long period when he'd stayed with his mother a lot, while she was sick, didn't help him get out and meet women, and some of the guys at work had given him a hard time about that—not out loud, but you could tell.

For a while, at Andy's Café, this guy around seventy brought his about one-hundred-year-old mother in for lunch every day. Carl had pictured them as himself and his mother—thirty years down the road—and had worried about that.

Now he figures he just needs some time to get to feel comfortable with somebody, and he is certainly comfortable with Anna—until she stands up. She's taller, by three or four inches. Anyway, now that his family's entire older generation has died except for Aunt Lil, his favorite aunt, the pressures to get married have actually eased up some.

BACK AT ROSEHAVEN, Faye Council, the physical therapist, holds the therapy room door open for L. Ray Flowers, her new favorite. He rolls in briskly, right leg propped straight out from his wheelchair. She is ready for his daily trick: after a strong shove on the wheels, he raises both hands as his wheelchair rolls toward the far wall. "Help! Help! Watch out, watch out!" He slows the wheelchair at the last minute, then maneuvers the chair back around to face her. "Howdy, Faye. What a day, what a day." A white, forward-and-back hair wave covers the front of his balding head. He is fair, almost red-complexioned, and thin-lipped. His quick black eyes are set so deep he sometimes looks cross-eyed.

Faye doesn't often take her work home with her, but the night before, over supper with her husband, Manley,

she related Mr. Flowers's version of his own life story—
a story he told quite readily: he grew up dirt-poor, one of
nine brothers and sisters in a Kinston, North Carolina,
churchgoing Pentecostal family, became an evangelist,
traveled to the Midwest, where he served, "pedal to the
metal, a-healing and a-squealing, a-touching and a-feeling."
He even preached to Faye the opening of a sermon that
came to him on the spot one time, standing at the pulpit.
He said that happened a lot—something real good would
just pop into his head. Then he'd go write it down and
memorize it for some other time. The sermon opening
was so different from any sermon she'd ever heard, she
wrote it down herself and read it to Manley there at the
supper table.

*"Listen. Be good to your feet. You walk on them every
day, if you're lucky. Don't be afraid to buy expensive shoes.
I'm L. Ray Flowers. I'm a prophet; I'm a snake. I'm a
salad; I'm a steak. I'm a gun; I'm a flower. I'm weakness;
I'm power."*

He was married once, then not married—enough said,
he told her. After he finished his calling out in the Midwest, he lived at the beach for a while, running a little
church near Dove, North Carolina, and almost got eaten
by sharks while fishing. Then he moved back to a small
plot of inherited land in Hansen County to recover, so
to speak, and started a furniture-building and -repair

business as well as a substitute-preaching business before (1) having his "final" heart operation—"Sir, we can't go back in there; it will kill you, I'm afraid"; (2) falling off a ladder while painting his shop gutters, severely injuring his knee; and thus (3) ending up at Rosehaven for physical therapy, which would be over as soon as he could bend the knee ninety degrees and also put his weight on it. And the sooner the better. The last place he ever envisioned himself, he said, was in a nursing home.

Faye told Manley how, at his second therapy session, Mr. Flowers asked her to move the exercise table against a wall so he could prop his feet high up, with his knees slightly bent, and then inch the foot of his bad leg down bit by bit. He'd learned about the use of gravity from moving furniture, he told her. She can't believe she'd never thought of that foot-down-the-wall trick—what a great idea. In fact, she plans to write up the technique for *JPT: The Journal of Physical Therapy*.

L. Ray's niece, Gladys Jenkins, whom Faye met in the hallway at Rosehaven, said to Faye on the day L. Ray was admitted, "All that stuff he did in the Midwest, all his nervousness and heart attacks and talking out of his head and stuff, is just the start of a slow brain rot that's being caused by him near about getting eat by sharks. Me and my husband, Gerald, we've just moved to Topsail Island, and I can't be bothered with him anymore at this late date in my own pretty dern frustrating life with my children and all. I've got enough to look after."

"Okay," says Faye, "if you'll roll over on your back, Mr. Flowers, we can finish our routine."

"You can call me L. Ray, Faye. All day."

Faye laughs. "Better not. Rosehaven policy. There. Now, let's get you positioned. Okay, that's good. Now, I've got to get over to Mrs. Osborne. I'll be right back. You know what to do.

"Okay, Mrs. Osborne, let's see if we can't lift this arm a bit here. Now, here we—"

"I got more problems than China's got china," says Mrs. Osborne. She lies on her back on a therapy table, looking—unhappy and worried—up into Faye's eyes.

"Well, we're going to work on some of them right now."

"Sometimes I wonder about people that don't have no problems. What do they do with their time? I wish I could come in here one day and say, 'I ain't got no problems,' just to see how it is."

"That's right," says Faye. "What would we do then?"

L. Ray listens. That'll make a good song title, he thinks: "Ain't Got No Problems."

OUTSIDE, CARL SITS in a porch rocker beside Aunt Lil while she smokes a cigarette. He scans the wide lawn, checks his watch. He needs to have that talk about her driving. He wonders if this is the time. Roman, the Rosehaven outdoor maintenance man, trims hedges at the front porch rail. Roman speaks only if spoken to. Carl has never seen him without sunglasses, outside or in. Mrs. Flora Talbert sits in her wheelchair by the door as if poured into a mold—a statue with moving eyes only. She has a large head, close-cropped white hair, and wears a pink housecoat. She also has a blue one and a yellow one. And a brown one that she doesn't like, because it's brown. She wears that one on gray, cloudy days.

Mrs. Talbert loves to look at shoes from her station by the door. Shoes tell a lot about the wearer. Some men's shoes have little tassels. Anybody wearing shoes with tassels likely has loose morals. And some of the shoes on women that sashay by show way too much skin—so much skin that they aren't even shoes, just straps. Mrs. Talbert is proud that all the shoes she ever bought for anybody in her family were good shoes, wholesome and solid. For men, a shoe without shoestrings is like a boat without a bottom.

BY THE OTHER SIDE of the door, backed against the wall in her wheelchair, sits Darla Avery. Darla is fifty-eight and knows she looks older. Much older. She is thin now but was overweight as a young woman.

She has diabetes, Parkinson's disease, and an immune-deficiency disorder that's so hard to pronounce, she doesn't try anymore.

And get this: a few days ago, she recognized L. Ray Flowers. He has not recognized her. Thank God.

It—the thing—happened in 1956, and that's all it was, what he did. She ain't over it and never will be. He looks a lot like he did back then, except for his white hair. He's now about, what, sixty-one or -two?

It was the eighth-grade end-of-the-year dance. L. Ray was in the shop class, and shop met with Mrs. Waltrip down in the littler cinder-block building where they had electric saws and everything. In assemblies and parties and trips and all that, shop—back before it was called special ed—was considered eighth grade. When eighth grade went on a field trip, shop went along.

Darla had been a friendly, overweight eighth-grader, not the depressed, withdrawn type. She was like Miss Piggy, in a way—sort of like a Miss Piggy cheerleader jumping in the air, tossing flowers out behind her. She was that kind of person, always very happy, with lots of girl-friends, always talking, always giggling about the boys, and always full of curiosity about who liked who and who was going steady.

And for the entire eighth grade, L. Ray kind of liked her. She could tell, but at the same time she wouldn't ad-mit it to anybody, because L. Ray was in shop.

She made good grades too, and teachers liked her. She was not bad-looking at all. She never had the first pimple, if you can believe that.

Oh, my God, there he comes in his wheelchair. Big as day.

L. Ray Flowers rolls across the porch, leg outstretched. Glances her way and nods. He doesn't recognize her. But who would?

Carl, sitting beside Aunt Lil, is deciding how to bring up her driving situation when up rolls the preacher, Mr. Flowers.

"Lord have mercy, Carl. Hello, Miss Lil," says Mr. Flowers. "I think I've stumbled onto a country song: 'Ain't Got No Problems.'"

"Carl has got a roomful of country song albums," says Aunt Lil. "He saw that movie . . . what is it, Carl?"

"*O Brother, Where Art Thou?*"

"Yes. How many times did you see that?"

"Four, so far."

"I heard about that movie." L. Ray turns his wheelchair a bit toward Carl. "Ralph Stanley's in that one, idn't he?"

Carl looks at Mr. Flowers. "He sure is."

"So you've got a few Dr. Stanley albums?"

"Yessir, I do."

"Do you have the one with the cross on the hill that has lightbulbs stuck in it all the way around?"

"I do." Carl notices Mr. Flowers gently touching his stiff helmet of hair with his fingertips.

"That's a good album," says Mr. Flowers. "I've done a little gospel music in my time. Out in the Midwest, I was preaching all over and couldn't get consistent music help, so I started a little group and we did right well. You play music?"

"Oh, no."

"You took those lessons," says Aunt Lil.

"That was a long time ago." Carl remembers his song-writing notebook full of half-written lyrics, only two or three complete songs—which all sounded alike when he tried to put them to music.

"Aha, here comes some more of my little congregation," says Mr. Flowers.

Along the sidewalk, from around the side of the building, comes—very slowly— two residents, Mrs. Maudie Lowe and Mrs. Beatrice Satterwhite, and an aide, Carrie Dillinger.

Suddenly the idea for that song, "Ain't Got No Problems," blooms full in Carl's head. Pop—there it is. A guy has a bunch of bad luck, gets thrown in jail or something, then gets out, and everything goes just the way it should. He suddenly has no problems. Things are going so well that when he tries to . . . when he tries to write a country song, he can't. There's nothing to write a song about.

Mr. Flowers says—bellows—"Welcome to the porch, ladies."

The aide looks like she's ready for a break.

Carl checks Mrs. Lowe's name tag. They are all required to wear them. He hasn't quite learned these ladies' names. Mrs. Lowe—Maudie—the very small woman. Her three-pod cane seems too tall, even though it's adjusted to the shortest height. He pictures her sitting down in a rocker, imagines her feet not touching the floor.

He thinks about his song again. The guy in the song finds a job, his girlfriend hasn't left him, his truck is not broke down, his lost dog is found. He'll start writing it after supper.

Beatrice Satterwhite, the large woman, big auburn hair with a gray streak, wearing a nice dress and a gold Victorian mourning pin, pushes her three-wheeled walker onto the stepless porch. The walker has handlebars and hand brakes—a Cadillac among Chevrolets, thinks Carl. He wonders if he should say that to Mr. Flowers. In the center of her walker is a sturdy, turndown leather seat. Carl has seen her roll it from inside the building straight to the porch rail, take a little U-turn, and instead of sitting in a rocking chair, fold down the walker seat, lock the wheels, turn around, and sit facing the lawn.

Unless he takes Aunt Lil inside, Carl figures he can forget about their little driving talk. He needs to be getting back to work anyway.

"It just stays very wide open," says Mrs. Lowe, "and very still, no matter what she's doing with her other eye. I guess it stays open when she sleeps at night." They have to be talking about the resident with the glass eye, a good buddy of Aunt Lil's, though Carl can't remember her name. . . . Cochran, that's it, Mrs. Cochran.

"I just wish she wouldn't talk so ugly," says Mrs. Satterwhite. "All that cursing. Once in a blue moon, I can understand, but she just don't let up, does she?"

"Well, Beatrice," says Mrs. Lowe, the little one, "you say that word for 'woman of the night' every once in a while."

"What word?"

"I'm not going to say it. When you talk about Walter Cronkite."

"That's not a curse word. That's just what they are."

"I think it is."

Mrs. Satterwhite begins to rock slowly, making little grunting noises. Carl wants to say something to either his aunt or Mr. Flowers, but he also wants to listen in case the other two start talking again.

"Did you say it stays open at night?" asks Mrs. Satterwhite.

"What?"

"Clara's eye—does it stay open at night, do you reckon?"

"I'm sure it does."

"No, she'll take it out at night."

"Not if she doesn't want to."

"I've seen them that look more real. They move and everything."

"It's like they put hers in but they didn't connect it to any nerves that can turn it."

"I don't think they connect it to the nerves, do they?"

"Well, they connect it to something, else it can't move around in there right along with the other one."

Aunt Lil is talking to Mr. Flowers about a squirrel almost getting run over in the driveway.

"Maybe they connect it to muscles," says Mrs. Satterwhite. "Nerves wouldn't be able to move it, would they?"

"Well, I don't know. They connect it to something."

"I know that. The question is, what do they connect it to?"

"I'm not a doctor. I don't know," says Mrs. Lowe.

Maybe there's a song in *here* somewhere, thinks Carl, but . . . maybe not.

"Looks like she'd just get a patch."

"Then she could get rid of the *eye*. You don't see people with glass eyes under their patches."

"Who can know?" says Mrs. Satterwhite. "I guess we'll have to go look it up in the encyclopedia. That's what they tell you to do in school. I remember doing a report on the presidents, and I found everything I needed in the encyclopedia. They have every one of them in there at one place or another."

"Probably under the letter their last name starts with."

They are silent. Then, "That's a funny word, *encyclopedia*," says Mrs. Satterwhite. "*Gymnasium* is a funny word too. There are lots of funny words, if you just think about it. . . . *La-boon* is a funny word and it's not even a word."

Mr. Flowers says he has to go inside and starts to move away.

"Mr. Flowers," says Mrs. Satterwhite. "Do you know anything about glass eyes?"

He rolls to a stop. "Glass eyes? Let's see. No, I can't say as I do."

"I wouldn't get Mr. Flowers involved in that," murmurs Mrs. Lowe.

Mrs. Talbert checks on the preacher man's shoes. Bedroom shoe on his outstretched foot is okay, but on his other foot is a tennis shoe, of all things. Men are wearing tennis shoes all over the place. A tennis shoe in a house of worship is worse than a worm in pudding. Or is this a funeral home? It's a nursing home. She knows that. She's not even supposed to be here.

"We can't figure out how you hook up a glass eye to the nerve endings," says Mrs. Satterwhite to L. Ray. "Do you know anything about that?"

Carl decides he has to go—at least stand up to go.

"But you can't see through a glass eye," says Mr. Flowers, smiling.

"I know that. But somebody said you could see through a glass eye darkly, didn't they? And besides that, I don't think the nerves will actually be wha—"

"The muscles, you mean," says Mrs. Lowe. "Something to move it. But how can you hook up something to a smooth, round ball, like a marble, that can move it around?"

"That's the sixty-four-dollar question," says Mrs. Satterwhite.

Carl looks at Mr. Flowers. Mr. Flowers is looking back at him with a gleam in his eye.

UNDER THE MIMOSA TREE, behind the fence, Carrie, the aide, sitting at the picnic table, smoking, says to Latricia Willis, another aide who's just come out and asked for a cigarette, "Did you hear what they talking about out there?" She reaches toward Latricia, holding out the cigarette pack, a cigarette shook up. She is tired.

"No." Latricia leans her back against the mimosa, one foot up under her against the tree trunk.

Carrie notices how slim and muscular Latricia is. "Mrs. Cochran's glass eye—they wondering what she connects it to."

Latricia lights the cigarette with a Bic lighter, her dark blue, white-striped fingernails almost as long as the lighter, takes a long draw, and blows smoke straight up. "What you mean? When she take it out? Put it on the table?"

"No. In her eye. In her eye socket."

"I thought you meant so it don't roll off the table," says Latricia. "What *does* it connect to?"

"I don't know. I hadn't thought about it. Ask Sabrina. She just got her medication certificate."

"I didn't know that."

"Oh, yes. She think she something now."

"I wouldn't hand out pills for nothing."

Carrie looks at her watch. "Well, I got to get back in there, change Mr. Anderson's dressing. That thing ain't ever going to heal."

"You can say that again. They'll be taking him off skilled care. There goes Medicare; here come Shady Rest."

"He'll be gone in less than two weeks, I bet."

The Kirby

CARL OPENS AUNT LIL'S apartment mailbox, under the outside stairway. She stands behind him in her walker. The box is stuffed with junk mail, three bunches wrapped with rubber bands—several "Have You Seen Me?" flyers, Citibank and other MasterCard and Visa inquiries, Home Depot sale notices. He sifts through the mail quickly to see if there are any get-well cards, although they pretty much stopped coming a while back.

"Don't you want to take the elevator?" Carl asks.

"No. I don't aim to start now. What have you got there?" Aunt Lil wears her green striped jacket over her blue sweat suit, a yellow scarf, and full makeup—all for this little visit to her apartment. She needs to clean some, she said.

"Mostly junk mail. You can look through it when we get upstairs."

"Lord, lord, all these card companies. What do they do with their time?"

"What do you mean?"

"Who sends all these things out? They won't allow the street panhandlers to beg, but the . . . damn banks can, through the mail."

He follows two steps below her, bringing up her walker. She stops on each step, holds to the rail. "See, I can do this all right," she says. Before she fell, she never stopped when she was going up or down, never put both feet on the same step.

Up top, he puts her walker in front of her, gets out her keys.

At the door she asks, "Is that the right key?"

"No, it's the wrong key. I thought I'd try a few wrong ones first."

She looks up at him, then smiles. One of her eyebrows is painted on higher than the other.

He follows her in through the door and turns on the air conditioner. He smells a tinge of cigarette smoke covered by the lemon freshener she's always used. She moved here after Uncle Tad died. It's a relatively old apartment building. In the living area of the large room sit her soft couch with the wooden arms, a wood coffee table, a big chair, a small chest of drawers with a writing desk built into the top, a TV, and another big chair with three welcome-mat-size squares of cut carpet on the rug to catch dropped ashes. A picture of red cherries in a bowl hangs over on the dining-area wall beside a certificate that reads "Lillian W. Taylor, Simmons Business School." Beneath the cherries and the certificate, a table holds family photographs.

He drops the mail on the round dining room table, sits on the couch, looks around. He doesn't have a lot of time today.

She stands in her walker. "I can get around without this walker in here. Don't you think so?"

"I think that will work all right. Keep a hand on something."

"I just want to look around before I do a little cleaning."

"You know, I can hire somebody to come in here and clean."

She touches the back of a living room chair, holds to it, moves and reaches to her TV chair, then to the back of a dining room chair. She slowly and carefully sits at the dining room table. "I know that. But I'm able to do a little cleaning."

Carl watches her as she picks up one of her cigarette lighters and looks at it, puts it back down, picks up another one. She looks all around, picks up her Washington, D.C., pepper shaker. He bought it for her on a Boy

Scout trip twenty-five or thirty years ago. He bought two, broke one, and gave the good one to Aunt Lil instead of his mother.

"Cigarette lighters," she says. "That picture of those cherries."

This is where I need to be, she thinks. And Carl needs to understand that.

"You said something about some more shoes," says Carl. "Do you want to check and see if there are some more shoes you want to take in?"

"Oh, yes. Shoes. I want to see if I've still got those bedroom shoes with the hard rubber bottoms. Something that won't be so slick."

She stands, steps into the kitchen. The pantry door is open: there are her canned string beans, pintos, corn, and plenty of other canned goods, a stack of paper bags, the broom she kept planning to replace, a dustpan. "I don't see why I can't move on back here. Do you?"

He was afraid she was going to ask that. "Well, I . . . no. We just need to try it a little longer at Rosehaven. You know what the doctor said." He steps into the kitchen with her.

"I don't like him. Do you?"

"Well, I don't know. It's hard to find a good one nowadays."

He looks inside the pantry, wonders what will become of all those canned goods—should he take them home?

Not yet. The doctor has said that only with full-time supervision should she live at home.

He shuts the pantry door, finds her in the hall, where her waist-high bookcase holds her three dictionaries, a history of Hansen County, a typing manual, a biography of Ronald Reagan, a book about Al Capone, three small bowls, and a copy of *Out of Africa,* the book with a cutout space inside—about the size and shape of a pack of cigarettes—where his uncle Tad used to keep cash.

She stands at the door to the extra bedroom. "You go up to the doctor's office, and you don't know which doctor you're going to see. . . . Let's check on them shoes. And I want to get my Kirby out. It's still in here, idn't it?"

"Yes. But that thing's too heavy for you to do anything with, Aunt Lil. Let's get your walker. We can't be too careful. Aunt Lil, wait a minute."

"Why?"

"I need to get your *walker.*"

Bringing the walker from the living area, he looks down the short hall, straight over her head. He remembers getting around behind her as a boy—at the sawmill where they'd go to get mulch—reaching up, grabbing her shoulders, holding on, riding her down to the soft sawdust. "Remember when we used to wrestle at the sawmill?" And in a flash, all that—the smell of sawdust, the morning coolness of it under his feet, the view down

through the pines, his mother and Aunt Sarah laughing—
all that comes back. He thinks about this apartment being empty of all the furniture, pictures. Maybe that time
is near. Maybe after she dies . . .

"Oh, yes," she says. "Lord have mercy. The old sawmill
—all the animals we buried there over the years. And I
could beat your hind end until you got so gangly."

. . . he can start his own business or something. At least
a new truck. But he isn't altogether sure how much
money she has, and he shouldn't be thinking about that
now. It's her money, and if all of it is needed to keep her
at Rosehaven, that's how it will be spent.

In this mostly empty extra bedroom, in the corner,
stands the shiny, mighty 1963 Kirby vacuum cleaner, fa-
mous because Aunt Lil traded it in for a new one twice
but each time took the new one back and repossessed the
'63. A table lamp sits on the floor, a big, rolled-up rug beside it.

Aunt Lil takes a few steps toward the closet, points.
"See if the Kirby implements are in there."

He opens the closet door. On the closet shelf sit ten to
fifteen rolls of toilet paper, three rolls of paper towels,
Fantastik, cans of Comet, jars of Pond's cold cream, and
all her vacuum cleaner implements.

She's over by the Kirby. "I'll roll it on out into the living room," she says.

"Let's go ahead and check for your shoes, and then I'll
vacuum the living room."

"I need to do it."

"Hang on until we get your shoes. Come on, let's just check on your shoes."

"Okay. But I need to do a little cleaning. That's why I came over here."

"I know. We'll do a little cleaning."

In the hallway bathroom—on the right—is the tub where she fell, got up, fell again.

In the big bedroom, many pairs of shoes are lined up on the floor over by her dresser. Her walk-in closet door is open: clothes hanging, metal file box on the floor.

On the wall in the bedroom is a photograph of Aunt Lil and three girls from her business school, all dressed up, standing on the courthouse steps, smiling, waving. The last time Carl and Aunt Lil were in her bedroom, she pointed to each girl in turn, named her, told a story or two about her, laughed, told about how the four of them had reunions every few years for a while after they graduated, and then they lost touch—except for Emma Brown, who runs A-1 Hair. Emma cut and styled Aunt Lil's hair until Aunt Lil went to Atlanta with a neighbor and bought two identical wigs. By then she was practically bald on top. Now both wigs look like their best days are gone.

She sits on the side of the bed. "I don't see any reason at all I shouldn't move on back home. They have those meals on wheels."

"Well, yeah, but what about your medicine? You know

we talked about that, and you remember how all that worked with Mother. It didn't go very well." Carl again visualizes this apartment empty, him sitting on the floor with his back against a bare wall. He feels almost overcome with some kind of blankness. He checks his watch. "I probably need to be getting on pretty soon."

"My file box is in that closet, idn't it?"

"Yes ma'am."

"I need to just check something out here for a minute or two." She stands, starts for the box.

"I'll get it."

"Okay. Suit yourself."

He senses that she wants to be alone with the box. "I'll put it right beside you, and I'm going to the kitchen to check out the pantry."

"Just give me a minute or two to see what all is in here."

At the dining room table, Carl looks through the mail again. The apartment is beginning to get cool from the air-conditioning. He clicks on the TV with the remote. Man, it took hours to teach her to use that thing. He'd have to get rid of captioning, or show her she was holding it upside down. Somebody will make a million dollars with the first TV remote for old people. Now they look like airplane instrument panels.

"Carl? Come here a minute."

He clicks off the TV. In the bedroom, on the bed beside

Aunt Lil, are a pile of war bonds, a coat, and a pair of scissors. "Great day. Were they all in your file box?"

"A few were, but the rest were in the lining of that coat. That's where Tad sewed them. He refused to spend money. Now, when I kick the bucket, you need to be able to put your hands on them."

"You got a while. You know that."

She picks up a bond and looks at it. Her hand shakes worse than he remembers.

"We shouldn't leave them in the file box, should we?" she says.

"I don't guess so."

"How about a safe-deposit box at the bank?"

"That will work."

"Count them, will you?"

He counts. It takes a while. "I get ten thousand three hundred dollars, and with the dates and percentages that comes to, let's see, around . . . well, it must be . . . I'll figure it later. It's right much. These are all from the early fifties."

"Tad wouldn't use the bank. Course, we never had a lot of money, but we did have these—and he kept buying them every once in a while. He didn't trust banks. Can you take care of this?"

"Sure."

"Put your name on the deposit box too. I remember Margaret and Sarah both had one. If we need the money for some reason, we'll cash them in. There's a paper bag in the pantry. Now, I need to vacuum."

"Everything's pretty clean inside, but there's some dust or old pollen and stuff out on the porch. I'll put the hose on the vacuum cleaner, and how about you do a little cleaning on the porch?"

"Well . . . okay. I can . . . I can do the rug later."

Carl puts the bonds in a paper bag, then goes back into the extra bedroom, disconnects the heavy floor attachment from the Kirby and puts it out of sight, finds the straight plastic hose with the brush on the end, and rolls the cleaner out into the living area. "Okay. Get your walker there, and follow me on out on the porch here and we'll . . ."

He unlocks and slides open the balcony door and heaves the Kirby over the bump. Heat engulfs him. The porch holds a small black metal couch and table and matching chairs; all are very dusty. He's going to have to tell Anna about this.

Aunt Lil follows him out, bumping her walker along.

He looks around. "Is there an outlet?"

"Right over there."

He plugs in the cord, hands her the hose, stands behind her and beside the Kirby. He presses the start button with his foot. It roars.

She reaches the brush attachment over her walker toward a chair and starts dusting and vacuuming. She turns, frowns at Carl, and points at the Kirby.

He cuts it off.

"This walker's in the way."

"Well, I don't know what to do about that."

"You can put it in the house."

"You need to keep your walker."

"Why?"

"Because you might fall."

"I'll be holding on to the hose."

"That won't keep you from falling, Aunt Lil."

"Well, how am I going to clean the porch?"

"I can clean the porch."

"This is my job."

"Okay, look. I'll put the walker inside, and then hold . . . hold to you while you vacuum." This is what a niece is supposed to be doing, he thinks. He opens the sliding door, sets the walker just inside.

He stands behind her, beside the Kirby. She holds the hose. He presses the start button with his foot, then holds on to a fistful of blue sweatshirt, pants, and diaper at her waist in back. She keeps her feet planted, sways slowly to the left and then over to the right, reaching with the hose, sucking up pollen. Then they move to a new spot.

After they finish, he stores the Kirby.

In the living area he checks his watch, then remembers. "What about your shoes? We forgot them."

"Yes. Yes."

"I'll get you a pair."

"I want to pick them."

In the bedroom, she picks a pair of bedroom shoes, a pair of dress shoes, and a dress and then asks Carl to take down her business-school picture. She'll hang it at Rosehaven.

GOING DOWN THE outside stairs, Carl leads the way, carrying her walker, the paper bag of war bonds, and the photo. He stops, turns, and looks up at her. She is stooped, holding to the railing, a sliver of diaper show-ing at her waist.

She looks down at him and frowns. "Why are you in such a hurry?"

"I'm not in a hurry. I've just got a few things to do." He is getting a little crazy. Now he has to go by the bank and rent a safe-deposit box. He did this kind of thing for his aunt Sarah, then for his mother, but neither of them had to go into a nursing home. Altogether, a goodly por-tion of his last ten years has been spent helping with their bank and personal business. He's pretty good at it by now. He thinks about some kind of business he can head up, where people with too little to do can be plugged into old people who need help. It would just take some organizing. He thinks about the problem of feeble el-derly wives who have only their elderly husbands to look after them.

"I used to come home," she says. "Now I visit home. I appreciate you helping me out."

"You're welcome. I'm glad to do it."

Lil thinks about all those bonds. Would they give her an opening to talk to Carl about her troubles with Tad? Maybe that is not such a good idea. When she gets a little worse off, maybe she'll tell him. Is there a good reason to keep all that from him? On the other hand, why bring it up now? Somehow she wants to tell him. But if she does, she's afraid she'll cry.

IN THE PARKING LOT, he folds her walker, then loads it, and her, into the car, and they head back to Rosehaven. He had planned to talk about her driving—while they were alone in her apartment—but he flat forgot. And she's seemed to back off the subject somewhat, hasn't mentioned wanting to drive again. Maybe she's made a private decision. Maybe he should let it ride for a while.

Darla's Flap and Snap

"I WROTE A SONG—the words," says Carl. He is in Aunt Lil's room at Rosehaven two days later, sitting in her Kennedy rocker, facing her.

She sits in her La-Z-Boy. "What kind of song?"

"It's a sort of country song—an idea Mr. Flowers had."

"Well, let me hear it. I like Mr. Flowers. He pays attention to everybody."

"I don't have any music yet. Maybe Mr. Flowers will write the music." Carl thinks of this as a joke, then considers it seriously.

"Well, that's just dandy. I'm glad he got in behind you. You've always wanted to do something like that, haven't you?"

"I think so. It was easy. It just sort of all came out at once. It almost wrote itself. In less than an hour."

"Let's go out on the porch so I can smoke me one. I'll bet he's out there."

It takes her two or three tries to stand. Carl moves her walker in front of her—she will allow him to do that. He knows what she will and won't allow: Help with coat or sweater, yes. Help to or from bathroom, no. Into car, no. Out of car, yes. Standing from an armless chair, yes. With arms, no.

The regulars are on the porch: Mr. Flowers; Mrs. Maudie Lowe, the little woman; Mrs. Beatrice Satterwhite, the three-wheeled-walker woman; the two silent ones by the door; and Mrs. Clara Cochran, the one who curses and has the glass eye. There are several empty rockers among them. Carl and Aunt Lil take two. Mr. Flowers sits off to the side, in the sun, reading a magazine. Carl sees *Furniture* in the magazine's title. On the flat, wooden porch rail beside Mr. Flowers is a red Bible, dog-eared, holding inserts and place-markers.

Carl is reluctant to mention to Mr. Flowers the song he's written, for fear of being too forward and then maybe of being kind of adopted by him, maybe talked to and talked to and talked to. On the other hand, he wonders if Mr. Flowers might be able to put some good music to the song, since he knows about traditional music.

Aunt Lil says, "A squirrel started crossing right out

there the other day, right there in the driveway, and here comes a car, and that squirrel goes this way and then back that way and then this way. It was the funniest thing."

"They need a squirrel safety patrol," says Mrs. Satterwhite.

"I was a grade mother for the safety patrol for nine years," says Clara Cochran. "I got so goddamned tired of Washington, D.C., I didn't know what to do. We took a trip up there every year."

"I wish you wouldn't use that language, Clara," says Mrs. Satterwhite.

"I don't know what I'd do if I had to stop driving," says Aunt Lil.

A silence falls.

"Well, it's something we all need to think about," Carl says to Aunt Lil quietly, so the others can't hear. Has he stumbled into the right opening? "Everybody has to stop sooner or later." He looks at her. She is staring straight ahead. He waits for a follow-up.

Nothing.

"Ha," says Mr. Flowers. "There's another song for you, Carl: 'The Safety Patrol Song.' Did you do anything with the one I gave you the other day?"

"I did. I wrote it. It just came all at once—the whole thing."

"Good. Let's hear it."

"I can't write music. I just did the words."

"Have you got them written down?"

"I do."

"Good. I'll put it to music. I wrote music for three Teddy Lakewood gospel songs. Did you ever hear of him?"

"Ah . . . I'm not sure. . . ."

"He went on to do some stuff in Nashville and wrote that gospel song that Buddy Arnault recorded: 'The Light behind the Clouds.' Did you ever hear that one?"

"I don't think so."

"Have you got your song words with you?"

"In the truck. I'll go get them."

Maudie is not especially happy to see the nice young man leaving. "Is he leaving?"

"He's just going to his truck," says Lil.

I wish that preacher would leave, thinks Maudie, and stay gone. He's too forward, especially for a preacher. "It's a beautiful day, isn't it?" she says.

"Yes, it is," says Beatrice. "They're all beautiful when you don't have any problems—like Mrs. Osborne. She says she don't have any problems. Idn't that what they were talking about?"

"I don't think she said that," says Clara. "She's more dead than I am." Clara does not fail to appreciate the cleanliness and finality about death—about death done right. Death isn't wasteful, unless you linger, and then it wastes time. But if you are lucky, it's a simple *poof,* and then you don't waste money and paper towels and water and food for another twenty years. Sometimes she thinks she is the only person left on earth who has a lick of sense about not halfway using things and then throwing them away. Why people don't have sense enough to hang up and dry out and reuse a paper towel, she cannot for the life of her understand. At the hospital they use everything once and then throw it away, lock, stock, and barrel. At Rosehaven too. Any fool can see that's wrong. The power belongs to manufacturers and office people and government people all over the globe, fools who don't have sense enough to use something twice, always busy wasting somebody else's money, then going home and doing the very same thing, not ever thinking about how much they waste every day. When her stepdaughter took over her household, all good sense about using and reusing went out the window, and Clara does not care to visit that house again in her lifetime. It would be too painful. Her daughter, not her stepdaughter, should have got that house, but her daughter was too proud to take it.

Beatrice brings her hand to her mouth and nose. "Whew. Who pooted? Whew." She speaks only loud enough for Clara and Maudie to hear.

"First smeller is the feller," says Clara. "Whoever smelt it dealt it."

Carl opens the spiral notebook, finds the new song,

and hands it to Mr. Flowers, feeling pretty confident that he will like it. "There you go, sir."

"Call me L. Ray. I ain't that old." He holds the notebook far from his eyes, pulls his glasses from his shirt pocket and puts them on, studies the lyrics, touches his hair with his fingertips. "That's great. Oh, that is just dandy. I'll get right on it." He hums a tune, changes it. "Yeah. Sure. No problem. I'll have something for you in a day or two. Now, do a safety patrol song next. Something funny, like this one."

"I was actually in the safety patrol."

"Who wadn't, that has any class."

CARRIE SITS UNDER the mimosa tree at the picnic table, on break. She opens a pack of four-cornered Nabs, concentrates on one before she bites into it. She is trying to forget the image of Mr. Felton's dry, open mouth.

Latricia joins her, leans her back against the tree, lights a cigarette, and asks, "Why it is Mrs. Talbert won't let nobody but you wipe her ass?"

" 'Cause she like me, I guess. It's just a phase."

"Traci says she asking for you all the time. She picky."

"Naw, it ain't that. I like her. She's got some spunk. She ain't got no sense, but she got some spunk—some left. I think it's 'cause she rich. She figure she can get whoever she want." Carrie looks at Latricia.

Latricia's eyebrows pull up and together. She looks back. "I can tell."

"Tell what?"

Latricia takes a draw from her cigarette. Blows smoke. "Tell what she thinking. I think she just a mean white woman."

"I wish I had your body and my mind."

Latricia drops her cigarette, steps on it, twists her foot. "Huh."

Carrie pushes another Nab up out of the cellophane and takes a bite, then drinks from her Diet Coke. "You better put that butt in the butt can. Mr. Rhodes'll be all over you."

"Mr. Rhodes ain't gon' do nothing."

Carrie thinks of Mr. Rhodes's big black car, all his businesses. Day-care centers, the Triple A Rent-All on Lawson Street, two hardware stores—one in Summerlin—three convalescent homes. Word is that his wife named them all: Bunny Bear Day Care, Little Rabbit Day Care, some other one, then Triple A Rent-All, Rhodes Hardware, Rhodes General Store, Rosehaven, Garden Rest, and that other one. . . . "What's that place he own on Gladstone?"

"Brook Arbor Gardens?"

"That's right. I can't ever remember it." Mr. Rhodes has given Carrie jobs at three of his convalescent homes. He likes her because she works hard, she guesses. "Mr. Rhodes, he gets 'em from the cradle to the grave."

"His daddy had 'em from the cradle to the grave."

"His daddy never owned all the stuff he own."

"I think he owned more."

Two helicopters fly over, one trailing along behind the other.

Latricia yawns, stretches. "Did you know Mrs. Osborne didn't use to wear no makeup?"

"Naw."

"That's what Faye says. Said she didn't wear no makeup to speak of till she had her stroke."

ON THE PORCH, sitting in the sturdy seat to her three-wheeled walker so she can get her money's worth from it, Beatrice watches as Roman, trimming hedges, stops his work, sneezes. "He's got a problem," she says.

"He coughs the way my husband used to," says little Maudie. "He's been dead over thirty years—thirty-some-odd years. His last job was on the board of trustees."

The movie starts in Beatrice's head. "Walter Cronkite gave me four thousand dollars, and that whore-hopping son of mine spent every cent of it in Reno, Nevada." The movie continues: Mr. Cronkite puts the money package into a big, blue U.S. Postal Service mailbox; a quick jump to her son standing in a doorway handing a fancy woman the first of many installments.

"You shouldn't talk like that about your own children," says little Maudie.

"Well, it's the truth. I have to tell the truth. Everybody does."

Carl stands and moves to the empty chair between him and L. Ray. Maybe L. Ray will have an idea on the driving problem. "I've got to tell Aunt Lil she needs to stop driving," he says, keeping his voice down.

"What's holding you up?"

"I don't know. I keep looking for a good opportunity."

"It's hard to lose your independence. My mama, back before she died, up at the driver's license bureau, couldn't tell what a stop sign was in the little picture machine. The patrolman or whoever wouldn't pass her. She got mad because the sign in the machine didn't have STOP written on it. It was just a shape, you know. She asked him if he'd ever seen a sign without anything written on it. He wouldn't talk about it and failed her, and then out in the parking lot she told me a friend of hers knew a place over in Burley County where it was easy to get your license, and about two weeks later she told me she'd gotten her license and said she wouldn't have to worry about it again until she was ninety-seven. Some of these ladies are pretty spunky."

Yeah, thinks Carl, and you seem to kind of go for them. "Aunt Lil tells me you played a song or two the other night."

"That's right. I'm doing a little Thursday-night gig until I get out of here."

"Mr. Flowers, go get your guitar," says Mrs. Satterwhite, leaning forward in her walker so that it scoots back about a foot.

"You better lock them wheels," says little Maudie.

"Yes, go get your guitar," says Aunt Lil.

L. Ray looks down at the magazines in his lap, sets them on the floor, puts his hands on his wheels, and turns to Carl. "Would you by chance go get my guitar?"

"Sure. What room?"

"Hall two. 202. It's on the bed. Here's the key."

In L. Ray's room, Carl sees a stack of magazines on the floor, the guitar on the bed. He looks at the brand name. Gibson. An old one. With the guitar, he heads back to the porch. He thinks about his guitar lessons, his song notebook, about the little Kay guitar his father bought him from Sears. He should have stuck it out.

Back on the porch, he hands the guitar to L. Ray, and says, "I took some guitar lessons about ten years ago."

"For how long?"

"Three months. I took three months of trumpet when I was in high school, and then three months of guitar when I got to liking bluegrass. I just can't stay with it."

L. Ray looped his guitar strap around his neck. "You should try bass guitar—electric. It's easy, if you've got any ear at all, and I'll bet you do. Can you sing?"

Carl starts to say no. He doesn't like his high voice. He'll sing along with the radio sometimes, though. Sing in the shower. "I sang in the church choir when I was growing up. But that's it."

"You sang all those good old hymns—'What a Friend,' 'The Old Rugged Cross,' 'Just As I Am'?"

"That's right." Carl remembers looking at his mother in the choir when the congregation sang "Standing on the Promises," how it was their favorite song together, how she would smile at him, and how he thought *promises* was a different way of saying *premises*, because "standing on the promises" made no sense.

"I'll bet that's part of what got you going on country music," says L. Ray.

"I guess."

"Well, ladies and gentlemen, here's one written by Dr. Ralph Stanley." L. Ray strums a chord, tunes his B string, turns his chair toward the others, and clears his throat. "One called 'Rank Strangers.'" Then he sings:

I wandered again to my home in the mountains

When he finishes the song, the group applauds. L. Ray sings two more. Then he takes a few minutes—studying Carl's lyrics on his knee—to work up a verse and chorus chord pattern. He interrupts the ladies: "Attention please." He strums a chord, then another, hums the first notes of a melody.

Then L. Ray sings the song, and Carl feels so good

about it—his and L. Ray's song—he is almost embarrassed. He wishes Anna had walked out on the porch and listened and then asked, Well, where'd that song come from? He knows it's a funny song. Mrs. Lowe and Aunt Lil actually laughed. They could make a CD. He wouldn't need that many more songs. But he doesn't want to show his excitement too much. Mr. Flowers is a little bit pushy.

Carl stands, and L. Ray holds out the guitar to him. "Would you mind taking this back to my room?"

At the main door, Mrs. Talbert eyes Carl's shoes as he walks by. Them Indian moccasin things, she thinks. They ought not be worn to church like that. They ought not ever be worn to church or to a funeral home. Men nowadays had rather shoot the moon than wear a pair of lace-up shoes.

DARLA AVERY ROLLS back inside when the music starts. She remembers the details leading up to the big event that night. They come to her one at a time as she rolls down the hall. It was so embarrassing, so awful.

And oh, was he ever more dressed up that night. Her mama and daddy were okay with him picking her up. Most anything was okay with them. Darla had lied to her mama, told her that L. Ray was in the tenth grade, which of course he would have been if he hadn't been in shop, because he'd flunked two grades. That man toting L. Ray's guitar passes her. They both think they are something, making music, when people all around them are dying. Making fun.

Back then, L. Ray had red hair, a kind of dark red, and his eyes had that quickness and he had that thin-lipped mouth that would always break into a big smile at nothing, right when he was looking so hard through those quick eyes.

He brought along a present when he came to pick her up, a brown leather billfold with the flap and snap and change purse and zip-up paper-money holder. It was in a box, wrapped up nice, with a big white bow and green paper. When the doorbell rang and she opened the door, there he stood with that green present.

Okay. Here is her room, 301. She needs to watch her program. It's probably already started.

AFTER CARL KISSES Aunt Lil on the cheek, L. Ray calls him over. "Listen, I've got an electric bass in the shop out behind my Airstream. Would you pick it up, by chance? Anytime."

"I don't—"

"My place is easy to find. I can show you a few simple patterns on bass and you'll be playing before you know it. I need some backup. And by golly, I think you're the man."

"I don't think I've got time to learn. I mean, I'd like to, but—"

"I'll just show you one song—one easy song—so you can say you know how to play bass in case somebody asks you sometime. It's a fine instrument. A Fender Precision, from back in the sixties."

"Well . . ."

"You take the first right, right up here after the McDonald's. That's Westview Road, and you just follow it as far as it goes. There are two forks; stay to the right. Go all the way to the end. The key is in a fake rock at the base of three walking sticks by the front door to the shop—there's nothing there but the trailer and the shop. The guitar and a small amp are in a room in back of the shop—the only extra room—straight ahead on the floor. Can't miss it. Bring the amp too."

The First Breakfast

THE FOLLOWING WEDNESDAY, on his long lunch
hour, Carl follows the narrow road to L. Ray's Airstream.
The road winds around and down, so that the whole
place can be seen from above. Behind the Airstream is a
tennis-court-size woodworking shop; a grown-over garden plot; several stacks of wood slabs covered by sheets
of clear plastic held down by bricks; a fire pit surrounded
by wide, flat boards resting end to end on stumps; barrels;
buckets; two refrigerators (meat smokers?); plastic chairs;
an orange plastic "danger" fence around a scrubby area
behind an outhouse; and a small sawmill. A broom leans
against the outhouse.

Carl is surprised that the inside of the workshop is well
organized and clean. The amp sits on the floor in the back

room, and lying on the floor, in an open case with yellow lining, is the honey-colored bass guitar.

AT ROSEHAVEN, L. RAY asks Carl to move books and magazines from the armless cane-bottomed chair in his room. "Have a seat there. I bought that guitar in 1968 when I was playing with my first gospel group. Everybody played guitar, so I bought the electric bass and played it for eight years on the road. I wore out three cases. Would you hand me that other guitar over there? I'll tell you, if I'd stayed in music and out of the pulpit, I might be a little farther along. Speaking of good songs, do you know 'Farther Along'?"

"Sure do." Finally, Carl thinks, somebody who knows the music *he* knows—but he also feels awkward. He can't remember being with a man in a room, alone. His father's face flashes before him. His father was a quiet man who spent most of his spare time in the little shop behind their house, which was usually off-limits for Carl. His father's name was Jacob. But nobody called him Jake.

L. Ray sits directly in front of Carl—face-to-face—so he can instruct. "Listen, before we start, I need to tell you about what happened yesterday." His eyes glow; he leans forward in his wheelchair. "This is big stuff."

The guitar feels heavy and solid in Carl's hands. He is ready to get on with his lesson.

"I was on the porch," says L. Ray, "with Miss Clara

and your aunt—what a duo they are—and they were talking about religion, and I got involved, and they came up with this idea, which I refined just a tad into this: a worldwide movement that will work to make churches and nursing homes interchangeable. Think about it: why should Christians, or anybody else, go to church on Sunday morning when they can go down the street to a nursing home and visit and gladden these wrecks of old women lining the grim halls of nursing homes?"

Carl thumbs the fourth string, then reaches over and turns the amp on. But he leaves the volume down because L. Ray is still talking.

"Look at all those ramps and empty rooms in every church in the nation—empty rooms all week long. Why shouldn't a few needy old people be staying there with church members taking care of them, in shifts? Or seeing that they're looked after. Let's see—in a very small church with a hundred and eighty members, each member would be on duty for two days a year. Doable. And there are churches out there with a *thousand* members. Why not? Practice what they preach. Why not? Why should churches and nursing homes not be interchangeable? Forever."

Carl looks up. L. Ray is staring at him—a half smile, raised eyebrows.

"Well," says Carl, "I don't know. I never thought about it." The room is feeling just a little bit smaller.

"This notion—this very simple idea—is where every religion on earth can intersect. Something every decent human being can believe in. I'm talking nursing homes interchangeable with synagogues too, and temples, mosques, whatever else."

Carl feels embarrassed, keeps his eyes on his thumb, which is on the top string of the bass. He doesn't say anything.

"Do you go to church?" asks L. Ray.

"Used to."

"Baptist?"

"Yes."

"And you left it?"

"Well, I don't know. I just . . ." He looks up.

"Are you a believer?"

"Yes. I am. But . . . What about let's play some music?"

"I can't think of nothing more Christian. And that's the genius of the idea. Idn't it?"

Was he talking about music or the idea? Carl wonders. "You know, I just—"

"I mean, Jesus will sure as hell be happy with it. I told Miss Lil and Miss Clara that they'd come up with a real certified revolutionary idea. It's just so simple and plain . . . and right! And I've got my first sermon on it right here." L. Ray turns in his wheelchair, grabs a yellow legal pad from the bed, drops it onto his lap, clasps his hands together, and looks up at the ceiling, then at the legal pad.

He reads aloud, as if preaching.

"I've been to the mountain; I've been to the valley. I've been to Mary; I've been to Sally. I've been to Peter; I've been to Paul. I've seen the river; I've seen the mall. Glory, hallelujah. And now I'm settling down to do one thing right, and lasting. We're going to make history. We are going to change the world."

There is something rhythmical about it, almost musical. It kind of flows. Carl looks up into the corner of the room, avoiding L. Ray's eyes. His voice is not unlike that of Mr. Dayton, the main preacher when Carl was growing up. But the words are sure different.

"Listen. Old people are still alive. Alive. Their corpuscles breathe and move like little tiny white things in tomato sauce. It's all any of us are given at the outset: life. It's all any of us lose: life."

Carl looks at L. Ray. L. Ray goes on reading.

"Now I'm a God-delivered, -sanctified, and -reformed preacher for the Wayward Traveler Map of Bethlehems, Buddha Gems, and Baptist Hymns. A lot of religions are wrong about a lot of things. All religions are right about a few things. And that's where our Rosehaven World Movement starts—where they all intersect: relieving the suffering of old folks at homes. We'll call it the First Breakfast, maybe.

"Oh, feckless, reckless Christians. Reward. Reward. Reward. Do your duties, go to church—do something,

anything—to get to heaven, the big reward. How child-ish! Selfish! How like a little boy! How babyish!"

Oh, man, thinks Carl, this is going to get him in trouble.

"There is—or should be—no victory except in work itself. Religion has killed stoicism; people had rather think right for heaven out of sight, than fight right for old people in plain sight, else old people wouldn't be lonely and sad in all these stinking places across the globe."

They sit, L. Ray reading, then staring at Carl, Carl nodding his head slowly, then eyeing the corner of the floor.

"I've got it mostly memorized. I can memorize a sermon. So now I've got to come up with a name for this movement—call it something completely different: Bob's Church for the Weary. The First Breakfast. I don't know. The Umbrella Religion for Easing Suffering among the Wrinkled. You know, whatever. It's just . . . just brilliant —the idea is—and I don't see why I can't launch the whole thing from right here. Do you?"

"I don't guess so." The man is just a little bonkers.

"And I think some of these old ladies will help me out, so I need to stay around Rosehaven for a while to get the thing launched. Let's play some music. The *movement* is going to need a little music. Whoa!" L. Ray closes his eyes, raises his right fist, tilts his head back: *"Besides playing the blues at the First Breakfast, O God in us all, we're going to invoke the spirits of Ralph Stanley, Mother*

Maybelle, Ernest Tubb, Bob Wills, John Prine, and Hank Williams. We'll have Carter Family nights, and we will sing out of the Broadman Hymnal till our heads fall off. Just a Friend We Have in the Old Rugged Rock of Ages."

A different slant for sure, thinks Carl.

"Praise the God in us all. Love Jeremiah, and feel sorry for Judas. In Judas, and at his pleasure, is the God in us all. He kissed Jesus and thus carried out the will of the God in us all, showed the failed human heart in us all. Love the Chinese; praise the Pygmies. Kiss the Aussies; bop till you drop. I am ready for a revolution. I am ready for a revolution of language, song, spirit, rock, sock, bebop, hip-hop, anthropology, morphology, geology, Scientology, holyology, holy water, dishwater, dishrags, and ragtime. Kiss my foot."

L. Ray lowers his arm, looks at Carl. "I've memorized a bunch of stuff. Now I can use it again." He hands Carl a sheet of paper on which he's written bass guitar tablature—the visual directions for where to fret the bass guitar neck for each chord L. Ray will play on his six-string. "You want to pick with your middle finger, not your thumb. Like this . . . there. That's right. And see, the basic setup is like the top four strings of a six-string. Do you know what an octave is?"

"Yes."

"You get an octave from here to two strings up and two frets, see? Good. You've seen tablature, haven't you?"

"Yes."

"All this is, is a kind of vamp, back and forth. That's right. You're quick. You just stay there in G. Listen to this —a song written by my old buddy Marvin B. Watkins. Okay, do that vamp there. Now on the chorus, where it starts," says L. Ray, "you've got:

> The right tool at the right time.
> Don't give me two nickels when I need a dime.
> The right tool at the right time.
> Scoobie doobie doobie do.

"Okay, right here you've got to go to an E minor, which is just four frets down from the G. I'd drop from the high G rather than the low one . . . good. Now come right back to G, then D, then G. Watch.

"Okay, now we go back to that first vamp, and I'll play a little break." L. Ray plays his old J-45 Gibson. Carl notices that he plays like Mother Maybelle Carter and Jim Watson—thumb on a bass melody run, with an index-finger strum. He plays and sings while Carl backs him up on electric bass.

Carl can hardly believe how easy it is. "It makes a difference if you learn an instrument while you're playing music you like."

"Well, yeah. It's kind of like a breakthrough. A 'Paul on the road to Damascus' kind of thing. It happened to me with some sharks."

"Sharks?"

L. Ray turns his guitar upright in his lap. "Yeah. Right. I'll tell you about it."

Not that I asked, thinks Carl. I want to play music.

"I was on this sandbar, fishing around an old ship-wreck. Me and three other guys. McGarren Island, Outer Banks. The great release: fishing. Jesus went after some fishermen, you know.

"And the tide starts coming in. Water up around our ankles, and then our knees, and the current is pretty strong, so somebody says, 'We better get on back.' Where we are, see," he says, describing with his hands, "is on this sandbar that you can get out to just during low tide —water up around your shoulders getting out there— and when the tide comes in, you have to swim back across. It's in Charlie's Inlet. We'd been doing that every day for two, three days. We were catching blues around that old shipwreck. In fact one of the guys was Marvin B. Watkins, the music man I was telling you about. We go fishing most every summer."

Carl wonders who he might go fishing with—what kind of group like that does he know? Well, there's Bobby, at work. He fishes.

"So Marvin B. swims back, then another, then it's just me and one more left. Guy named Skip Hodges. And everything's fine.

"Then they holler at us, scared-like, and I turn

around . . . and see two black-gray fins cutting along behind us. You can almost see, you know, scars on them. Ugly things that made you see the red dust of the sacred stars in a far corner of the universe. And the thing is, we'd been cutting the throats of those bluefish, to bleed them. So I suddenly realize there's all this blood floating around us, and we're amongst sharks. My legs go a little weak and ice water runs down my back."

Carl wonders if somebody has taught L. Ray to talk the way he does.

"We start pulling fish off our strings like crazy and throwing them out toward the shipwreck. This is all work, no play. I'm concentrating on my fish string and I lose sight of the fins. Then I hear somebody holler, 'There's more than two!' We got a whole choir of sharks around us, see?

"So Skip gets his fish throwed away because he hadn't caught that many, and he starts swimming back, with the others yelling, 'Don't splash! Don't splash!'

"I glance at him. I'm still throwing away fish. God, take my fish away—clean the water of blood. Lift and deliver my sweet, fat fanny to shore.

"Well, Skip don't have a shirt on, and he's swimming a kind of a dog paddle, with his rod in his teeth—the little end—sort of dragging the reel along behind him. And I don't see no fins. Anywhere. God, hear my prayer.

"I suddenly realize I can sort of sling the whole string

of what's left, maybe three blues, away from me, so I do, but they don't go far. They're just starting to sink and *whap!* They're gone."

"A shark."

"Right. I toss my rod and reel and head for the kind, white sand of shore, swimming the sidestroke, trying not to splash, knowing I've got to swim across this deep part, realizing I should have kept the rod in case I need to poke at them or something. Then I'm up over the deep part and picturing in my head how deep it is, and picturing them grinning, coming up, eyes on my legs, when all of a sudden I think, My T-shirt's got blood and bait all over it. So I stop swimming and my legs drop down, and I get the T-shirt off and sling it back behind me as far as I can, without looking, and in about two seconds I hear this"—L. Ray slaps his hands together—*whap!*

"And then I'm swimming sure enough, sidestroke, and I'm thinking if I can just get to knee-deep, if I can just get to knee-deep, O God, my Savior, where I can stand up. And then there I am, about waist-deep. I stand and start striding as carefully as I can, not splashing, then I'm knee-deep and I start running, lifting my legs real high, and then I'm on the sand and I sit down with the others. And here's where I cried and cried and cried.

"So for weeks after that I wasn't right somehow. God was no longer somebody I had a phone line to, God was more . . . I don't know, very different. Because I didn't see it like God had saved me. I knew he hadn't. What had happened was the sharks just didn't hit me. Period. End of remarks. It had been up to them, not God. I saw that —clear. And so I was a wanderer for a while, until I had my last heart operation, and they told me it'd be the last, and while I was recovering from that, I got to reading some, and it's been all new and pretty strange and fun since. When I think about it, right this minute, I think all this has been a kind of preparing for Rosehaven, for this movement."

"That was a pretty close call."

"It was. Now onward and upward. Next Thursday, me and you is playing a little gig for the ladies, in the lobby. Lobby the ladies in the lobby library. Or maybe in the activity room. It's already on the calendar. We can practice a couple times more. And I might have to say a prepared word or two after we do a little music—about the movement. Are you with me?"

"I guess so. With the music anyway." Carl feels himself pulled along a little faster than he intended, but the whole idea of performing a song he's written, cowritten, is something else, different, new, secretly dreamed of.

"You take that bass with you. I don't need it anytime soon. You're a natural. And didn't you tell me you used to sing in a church choir?"

"When I was little, but I—"

"Can you sing harmony?"

"I guess. But I'm not much for singing." Carl looks at his watch. L. Ray will probably want him to sing high tenor, and that's not something he wants Anna to hear. He's been practicing relaxing his vocal cords. "I've got to stop in to see Aunt Lil and then head on home, but I appreciate you showing me this."

"Don't you want to take the bass and amp?"

"Well, no, I . . . okay."

"Take that book of songs over there. That's a good little book. The ones I do are checked in the table of contents, and I've gotten tablature written out for the first three. And see if you can work out a harmony part for the choruses—a high harmony would be great. But only if you feel like it, and on 'Ain't Got No Problems' the harmony should be simple."

IN THE BEDROOM of his small apartment, Carl opens the guitar case, takes out the guitar, and slings the strap around his neck. He turns and faces the mirror. Maybe the guitar should be a bit lower. He can reach the strap buckle. He adjusts it. He doesn't even have to take it off. Now it's lower. That looks better. He plugs the cord into the guitar, then the amp. Plugs the amp into the wall outlet. Stands back in front of the mirror. His thumb rests on the fourth string. He switches to his middle finger. Yes, that looks better. He plays a note, reaches over, turns the volume up a notch. He starts playing. Then he starts singing, "Way downtown, fooling around. Took me to the jail. Oh, me . . ."

He likes what he sees in the mirror.

Part 2.

Thunder Road

Stand Up and Boogie

IN THE ACTIVITY ROOM, Carl sets his chair facing a half circle of tan folding chairs. L. Ray will sit beside him in his wheelchair. He sets the small bass amp beside his chair and moves another chair from the back of the room. That's where he'll place his "cheat sheets"—notebook paper with tablature. He checks his watch. He is nervous, sweating under his arms. He was afraid of that and has worn a white shirt so the perspiration will show less. He figures there is little chance Anna will be around to hear, though, this late.

L. Ray rolls in, his guitar across his lap, a yellow legal pad resting on top of the guitar, and stations himself beside Carl's chair. "I've got a little sermon written out," he says.

At about 7:20, Aunt Lil, Mrs. Satterwhite, and Mrs. Cochran, pushing their walkers, find their way to seats. They are dressed up. A few minutes later, Carrie removes two chairs from the half circle, and into that space she rolls Mrs. Talbert, dressed in her blue housecoat. Several others wander in at about 7:25.

At 7:35, L. Ray says to Carl, "Let's start in with just the music."

"Wildwood Flower," instrumental version, for a nursing home audience, it seems to Carl, is wildly received. Everyone applauds briefly. Clara Cochran says, "Yahoo!"

It seems to be a good shoe night to Mrs. Talbert. She wonders where her friend is—the one who sits on the other side of the front door and has started talking some about the preacher man.

"We're happy to be here, ladies," says L. Ray. "I've got me a new sidekick to help out on the music tonight, Carl Turnage, and before we get to a brief message, we'd like to do a couple more songs. That was a song many of you may recognize, 'Wildwood Flower.' Next up is a little ditty that my sidekick, Carl, and I put together after being inspired by Mrs. Jenny Osborne."

There are a couple of snickers.

"So let's have a hand for Mrs. Osborne." L. Ray points to the rear of the room.

Mrs. Osborne had rolled her wheelchair in during "Wildwood Flower" and parked it against the back wall.

She hears the applause and sees heads turn to look at her, but she doesn't know why. She is thinking. She tried to stand in therapy earlier in the day and failed, and she's wondering if she should try again tomorrow, or if they will let her wait a day or two. She wonders where the next place she'll go will be.

"It's 'Ain't Got No Problems.' A one and a two and a . . . " L. Ray starts in with a Travis pick on a C chord. Carl joins in on bass.

> I got thrown in jail last summer,
> Beat up by a jailhouse mob. . . .

Carl follows along on the printed tablature, aware that this is his song, his words. He feels he is inside a dream that has nibbled at him for ten years at least.

"Will the Circle Be Unbroken" comes next, with Carl singing a tentative tenor on the chorus. They finish, and as the applause spatters out, Carl stands, rests the guitar in its stand, and starts for an empty seat. There, out in the hall, stands Anna, smiling at him. He turns his back to her and sits down, feeling a trickle of sweat run down his side. Where did she come from? What did she think of all this?

"I'd like to deliver a brief message," L. Ray says to his audience, moving to get comfortable in his wheelchair, his bad leg extended. He raises his hand. "I feel the Spirit upon me. And I must tell you at the outset here that Mrs.

Olive and Mrs. Cochran in conversations on the porch have provided me with an idea that I think is truly revolutionary. We can please Jesus, and please every religion's leader who ever lived, by working to accomplish one single task: making churches and nursing homes interchangeable. It's that simple."

Somebody sneezes.

Carl glances over his shoulder. She is gone. He looks back at L. Ray.

L. Ray tilts his head back and, glancing now and then at his legal pad, starts softly, almost as if praying.

"I have changed. My life is renewed, reborn, in a fit of unexplained crying after I almost got eat up by sharks. If you don't believe in rebirth, you don't believe in life. If you don't believe in life, you don't believe in death. If you don't believe in death, you don't know how to live. If you don't know how to live, you will die without living. If you die without living, you lost your chance. If you lost your chance, you missed the boat. If you missed the boat, you ain't sailing. If you ain't sailing, you're sitting. If you're sitting, you need to stand up and boogie."

Carl notices a steady increase in . . . in energy, volume.

"Boogie-woogie glory be to every whap-whop jack-junkie honky-punkie snip-snap-snay foy-fey lard bucket caught in the grip of greed. Shout it out. Strike down, O Lord God, Jerry Falwell and Pat Robertson, Jimmy Swaggart and Norman Vincent Peale. All the TV preach-

ers in the land, sentimental slobs who have called on the syrup of sweetness to suck up money from the more sentimental than they are, to lead human bleating sheep to the slaughter of dreaded dullness and sameology while jerking Scripture from an ancient context into the blur of a modern need to control and be right—to control sheep sitting on their couches on their white cotton wool heinies, buying . . ."

"Amen," says Clara Cochran.

Carl becomes aware of how well L. Ray is holding the ladies' attention. All of them. He is almost singing now.

". . . into avarice, the greed of seeking reward, seeking salvation, seeking the reward of salvation, seeking words to promote narrowness, selling the package, talking carny talk, shunning real work, real work for the real relief of real suffering. Victory is in work. What good is heaven, what good is enlightenment to a kind, lovely lady in a nursing home for whom 'home' is a field pea on Mars? I am into the first step of the First Map of the First Breakfast. And what we are about to do, ladies and gentlemen—now stop, look, and listen."

L. Ray stops, looks into the eyes in front of him.

"We are about to pronounce the grand fact that nursing homes and churches all across this land must become interchangeable. Why do we need a church house for Christians to visit on Sunday mornings when we've got nursing homes for Christians to visit? Christians sitting in

churches while nursing homes sit around the corner is wrong! "

"Amen," says Mrs. Cochran. "That's what I said."

"I think that's what I said," says Aunt Lil.

"*And why do we need nursing homes when we've got vacant rooms in church buildings? We need not two institutions such as these, going about instituting institutional double time. We need one. And it shall be called Nurches of America, Chursing Homes of the United States. I'm not saying we can take care of the very sick. But we can take care of the very poor and the very lonely. And all religions, all good people, all noble people, all noble old people, will get behind this bandwagon, which as of tonight, July sixth, 2000, is under way from this half circle of chairs in the activity room of Rosehaven Convalescence Center, Hansen County, North Carolina, United States of America, Earth, World of the God in Us All, amen, and amen, and we will see in the generation of our great-grandchildren Nurches of Mother Earth with Earthly Mirth, praise the God in Us All, thank you very much.*"

He begins to wind down. Carl looks at Aunt Lil, the others.

"*In closing, we've got to work against all the silly sissifying of so-called religion in America. And these, my loyal friends, are just words, lifeless without the help of the God in us all. We need to plan a First Breakfast. We've had the Last Supper for these two thousand years.*

*Now, in the spirit of rebirth, we also need a First Break-
fast plan. We need a hand-me-down-my-walking-can-
do-it plan. We must embrace the love of neighbor and the
give-love spirit of all religions. Here at Rosehaven, here
at the first First Breakfast, we will have sons and daugh-
ters of the Last Supper, and we will soon hereby christen
this new movement something like this—I don't know
yet: the Inclusionist First Breakfast Church of Jacklegs,
Jesus, All the Rest, and Baptist Hymns Which Are the
Best. Amen. And now let us each say a prayer in our
hearts, each for the other, and for the noble old here
among us and across the land. May we bow our heads for
a moment of silent prayer."*

"O dear God," says Beatrice, "Walter Cronkite gave
me four thousand dollars and that whore-hopping son of
mine spent every cent of it in Reno, Nevada."

Aunt Lil whispered, "Beatrice!"

"Bless you, Miss Beatrice," says L. Ray.

"God bless America," says Mrs. Talbert. She starts a
slow roll out of the activity room and toward her room.
She is ready to go. She has had a very careful look at the
preacher's shoe. It's some kind of brogan, she reckons.
She won't count the bedroom slipper. What is a brogan,
anyway? It has laces. She knows that. On his good foot is
a nice brogan lace-up, and because he is sick, he didn't
have to wear that if he didn't want to. That showed character. She thinks she might like this man. But what is a

brogan for, working or church? What is a brogan anyway? *Brogan.*

"Mrs. Talbert," she hears the preacher say. "We've got
a short meeting before we leave. And two more songs."

"I'm out of here, thank you," she says. She has heard
all she wants to hear—he really is a preacher, after all—
and the big clock on the wall says eight o'clock and she
has to be in bed by eight-thirty and it takes her a while
to manage, and the aide on duty doesn't always come at
just the right time. Sometimes they come early and sometimes late. Ah, there is someone, an aide, behind her, to
push her on home. She looks over her shoulder. Carrie.
Good. Carrie is on second shift. Strong hands to push her
on along in the hallway, where there is a slight chill in the
air. And there is Darla.

BACK IN THE ACTIVITY ROOM, after the program,
Clara Cochran comes forward, pushing her walker, to
shake Mr. Flowers's hand. Here is some damn flash and
excitement, for a change! A man who by God says what
he means and means what he says. And this man has a
plan to finally do something about nursing homes. "Mr.
Flowers," she says, "congratulations. I'm behind you one
hundred percent."

"Mrs. Cochran, thank you. I'm excited about what
we're about to get under way."

Lil stays in her chair. She is a little bit confused by Mr.

Flowers's message. But she can ask Carl about it. She is wondering if she's supposed to do something—if she's been chosen as some kind of disciple. She was unable to concentrate on the sermon, on exactly what is supposed to happen across America, because she kept thinking about Carl—how this is such a good opportunity for him! Even if it is gospel music. She remembers when he sang with the junior choir in church. She'd go to hear him when he sang. It had been too stiff for her, somehow, though she never said that to her sister, of course. The Baptists were just so *sure* of themselves about alcohol and dancing and went on and on about it. She can't understand why they say the Bible says this and that, but skip wherever Jesus drank wine. They were able to block out what they didn't want to hear. Then again, she wished Tad had been a Baptist and hadn't got into drinking the way he did, and then all that other business. Sometimes she wishes she hadn't found out what she found out.

Anyway, she went to a Methodist church for a while, a church that seemed a lot softer and easier, but just as sincere. And then Tad came along and he wouldn't go with her. Her mother had that spell of being "saved" and then got over it, but Margaret wouldn't ever turn it loose. In any case, Lil had gone to hear the junior choir when Carl was a member, and he was so cute up there with a white shirt and tie, singing away. They all, the three sisters, had such high hopes for him. And then he ended up kind of normal, in the awning business, even though she, Lil, had been almost certain that there was something for him in the world of music—he loved collecting albums so well and had taken guitar lessons.

She looks around for him. Surely he hasn't gone home without sitting on the porch with her while she smokes one.

WITH HER BACK against the wall, in her chair just outside her room, Darla watches as people come out of the activity room.

Even though he was in shop, he seemed pretty smart to her, and back there in the days when boys combed their hair, he combed his very nicely. Dark red hair.

And then in high school he was in regular classes, and he was always talking to people, patting them on the back, laughing out loud at his own jokes, making fun of people in nice, very acceptable ways and all that. He actually had a kind of adult presence about him. She always did feel there was something a little bit strange about him, but because he liked her, she overlooked that feeling.

On that night of the eighth-grade dance, L. Ray was standing there on her porch in a light gray suit, white shirt, bow tie, and black shoes, holding that green present with the white ribbon, and he gave a little bow with his hands under his chin like a Japanese, which is something she forgot—that Japanese bow. Just about anytime

L. Ray came up to you and spoke, he'd do that—do a little head bow with his hands in prayer fashion below his chin.

Of course she was wondering if he'd try to kiss her good night, but in the main she was seeing that particular night as the beginning of a high school career of dates and fun times. For some reason, she hadn't connected being overweight to being unpopular with the boys. That didn't dawn on her until later. After all, L. Ray was a boy and had been interested—or at least a little interested—in her for a whole school year.

She wore her sister Glenda's blue crepe dress with the silk top and frilly bottom and fake pearls and earbobs and lots of lipstick and eye makeup. Glenda was seven years older than her and already married then.

He opened the passenger-side door for her. It was his daddy's Oldsmobile . . . or Pontiac, one of those big ones with a lot of chrome, but it was very old and worn-out looking also. L. Ray's daddy sold eggs.

She remembered he pulled the car into the Blue Light, a main nightspot back then, to get cigarettes. And then he'd said, "How about we stop back in here after the dance for a couple of tall Busches?"

Darla and Linda McGregor had drunk beer together twice. Darla was ready to bop. There were lights in her eyes. Blue lights from the Blue Light. Red lights from the cigarette she was about to smoke. White lights from the dance. Green lights from the dashboard of the car when they drove off somewhere later, maybe out to Lake Blanca. She knew a lot about life. She had sat in the back row at the movies with Diane Coble more than once. When Dwayne Teal would come in, Darla would quietly watch them out of the corner of her eye. They would make out during the whole movie. Not to speak of what she'd seen Glenda and her boyfriends do sometimes when Mama and Daddy were gone.

So they arrived, after each having smoked a cigarette on the way.

The dance was in the library. L. Ray parked the car by the tennis courts in back, and they walked around to the front of the school and up the high brick steps and in through the doors and then down that long, long wood-floored hall. She hasn't seen a hallway with a wood floor in thirty years.

Here he comes out of the activity room, leg out straight, rolling along, laughing.

At her desk, Anna is finishing the notes for the next day's care-plan meeting. The staff will consider whether or not to downgrade several residents from "skilled" care. Mrs. Osborne's case is coming up. A resident's downgrading will doom their Medicare, of course, and a strong case has to be made either way.

"You're putting in mighty long hours." It's Carl at her door. She can hardly admit that she has hoped he'll stop by. His voice seems lower than usual.

"I left two files here," says Anna, "and so when I came back and found them, I decided to stay to finish up. We've got a care-plan meeting tomorrow, which means lots of important decisions. And Mr. Rhodes is going to be here, the owner. He comes to only a couple or three of these meetings a year. He probably ought not to know about Mr. Flowers's movement."

"Why?"

She wishes he'd come on in and sit down. "He's very religious and probably won't like the sound of it. I've just got a feeling he won't. But Mr. Flowers is not going to be here that long. Except his physical therapist says his knee has suddenly gone stiff on him. She's planning to call his doctor."

"I won't say anything to Mr. Rhodes," says Carl, "but some of the ladies might." He concentrates on keeping his voice pitched low.

"We'll just have to see. Looks like your guitar lessons are paying off."

"I guess." Relax the vocal cords. Relax the vocal cords. "Looks like I'll be helping Mr. Flowers with some of his programs."

"Do you have a cold?"

"Oh, no."

"How many songs do you all know?"

"Not too many. Actually we're writing a few together."

"He mentioned that. I heard the one about problems."

" 'Ain't Got No Problems.' Right. We worked up that and 'The Safety Patrol Song.' Were you ever in the safety patrol?"

"No. We didn't have one of those."

"Oh, man. That was a big deal at Hansen Junior High. White strap, the works. We had these inspections, and your strap had to be real white. We had some kind of paste to whiten it with, I remember. And right now I'm working on the words to a song called 'How Come I Miss You When You're with Me All the Time?' L. Ray got the idea from somebody on the porch, just like he did the others, passed it to me, and I'm doing the words. He'll do the music."

"I'll bet. And he does all those old gospel tunes."

"Yeah, we started working on 'Angel Band.' Same as in the movie *O Brother, Where Art Thou?* Have you seen that?"

"No."

A fountain erupts in Carl's head. "Want to go?" He immediately regrets asking.

"Well . . . well, yes."

"Then I guess they're not your children, are they?"

"Carl—actually, they are. I've been divorced a little over a year."

"Oh. I see. Well, the movie. How about Saturday night?"

"Okay. Cool."

"Great."

Carl turns—too abruptly, he knows—and walks away. He can't believe he didn't even say good-bye. He hasn't had a date in three months, since Teresa Suggs. "Good night," he says to Carrie, standing by another aide stationed at the front desk. Is her name Latricia?

LATRICIA, TAKING OVER night desk duty for Traci Cox, listens as Carrie tries to explain something about a note in the activity room, above the microwave.

"Well," says Carrie, "if you don't think it's funny, just come down here and look at it."

"I seen the sign, Carrie." Latricia doesn't want to walk any more than she has to. Not now. She'll be in the halls all night.

"But not with that line through Miss Suzanna's name."

"What's so funny about that?"

"I can't explain it. Just come look."

"Is this some kind of trick?"

"No."

A sign in the activity room, taped to the wall above the microwave, reads:

> ### PLEASE! ! ! ! !
> DO NOT USE MICROWAVE WHEN
> ANY OF THE FOLLOWING
> ARE IN THE ROOM:
>
> PEGGY JOHNSON
> GERALD SWENSON
> MAUDIE LOWE
> ~~SUZANNA DAMPIER~~
> BETTY WISE
> VIRGINIA MCDONALD

"See that?" says Carrie.

"I been seeing it for three years."

"But not with a line through a name like that."

"She went home."

"I know that, but it look like the microwave killed her."

"What's so funny about that?" Latricia scratches behind her ear with her long blue-and-white fingernail.

"Did I say I wish I had my mind and your body?"

"I think you probably did," says Latricia, turning and heading back to the night desk.

ON THE COUCH in their living room, Faye Council is telling her husband, Manley, about the preacher's plan. "He was practicing on me yesterday afternoon in therapy—this sermon. It goes all over the place. Going to change the world. He preaches like some of them old-timers on the radio, and he's going to lay it on the line tonight." She looks at her watch. "Already has."

"Hand me that remote," says Manley.

CARL MOVES HIS RADIO into his bedroom, then sits on the side of the bed with the bass guitar across his knee. He turns the radio on, adjusts the volume, finds 92.3 FM, the bluegrass station, and listens. The third song he recognizes; he finds the key, B, and starts playing. It's fast, but he is keeping up. It goes from a B down two frets and then back up to a B. He is playing along. He stands, looks at himself in the mirror. "Yonder stands little Maggie," he sings. He gets off somehow, but then gets back in. It doesn't sound great, what he's doing, but he still likes the way he looks with the guitar hanging around his neck, kind of low at his waist. He stands, waiting for the next song.

Mr. Flowers Needs to Go

CLARENCE RHODES IS FURIOUS. He drives over the speed limit—rare for him. A phone-mailbox message, in a voice he didn't recognize, has just told him that an L. Ray Flowers is starting a religious cult at one of his convalescent homes. Clarence remembers the name from twenty years ago or more—something in the papers about IRS problems or something.

Clarence will go straight to the horse's mouth, something he is good at. He will talk to Flowers. Rosehaven is about to be sold to Ballard College, and this cult business is just the kind of thing that could turn Ted Sears, the college president, away. Sears is a solid Christian, and Rosehaven is going to be a good place for Sears to retire some of their donors to, elderly, rich donors, mostly old ladies whom Sears and his men have—what's the word? —*asked* to donate their life savings to Ballard. A Ballard lawyer prepares wills and trusts, while others at Ballard provide services such as lawn mowing, painting, nursing care. There have been a few lawsuits about it, but they don't go anywhere, of course. What better use, what more Christian use of an old person's money, than for the Christian education of America's youth? Those children who have sued are just showing the world what kind of selfish, mealymouthed offspring they are. If they'd taken care of their parents, their parents wouldn't be leaving their money to Ballard. Kaput. Simple as that. And now, just as his people and Sears's people are nearing agreement on a price, here's this L. Ray Flowers character. What in God's name is he up to? You can never tell about a Pentecostal. You can never tell. Fringe stuff.

He pulls into the parking space marked DOCTOR. It's always empty.

And there sits Anna behind her desk, poring over notes. Clarence wishes all his workers were as dedicated. "Hello, Anna. Which is Mr. Flowers's room?"

Anna stands. "202, sir."

"Do you know anything about him starting a religious cult of some sort?"

"I don't think it's a cult, Mr. Rhodes. It's more some kind of movement he's dreamed up."

"Movement?"

"Something about making churches and nursing homes interchangeable. That's all I know. I don't think it's going to amount to much."

"What is he . . . ? I need to talk to him. We don't need his kind of church work. I'll be right back." He starts down the hall, stops, returns to Anna's office, sticks his head in her door. "When is he scheduled to be out of here?"

Anna stands again. "Theoretically, as soon as he can bend his knee ninety degrees and walk comfortably. His niece is working with a neurologist to get a recommendation for him to stay, I think—something about some seizures a few years ago. She thinks he has mental problems. The ladies like him, I can tell you that. He sings gospel music and funny songs, and—"

"I'll be right back. I just need to find out what's going on."

Clarence has never had a better social worker than Anna. And she is so attractive. So efficient. He'll actually go out of his way to stop in and talk to her. And she always seems to know what is going on everywhere in the building. If he were to create some kind of assistant CEO of Caregood, Inc., she would be the one. A woman, at that. No problem. And she always has that twinkle in her eye. One reason he is able to keep her happy is his own concern for the elderly, his own understanding that he is answering a call from God. He runs a good, clean, wholesome business, a business that at base relies on the foundation of family, the sanctity and sacredness of the family. The family—an institution that seems doomed by a greed-driven entertainment industry run by weak-kneed, infidel sniff-heads the nation over. And yep, his nursing people wear caps and uniforms. One of the best ideas he ever had. It makes the old people feel safe.

L. Ray is under a lamp, rewriting a sermon. He has finished five now, and figures about twelve will be needed to launch his movement. He is trying to think of a word other than *seven* or *eleven* that rhymes with *heaven*. *Leaven?* As in *leaven bread?*

Two hard knocks on the door.

"Come in." The door opens and there is Rhodes, the fellow who owns the place, looking like he always looks —busy. What does he want? "Mr. Rhodes. Come in, sit down—just put that stuff in the chair on the table there. What can I do for you?"

"Mr. Flowers," says Rhodes.

L. Ray takes the extended hand; it's big for a relatively short man. Rhodes is dressed up in a navy pin-striped suit with a white shirt and a red tie. His big face is flat and pale. He's got cancer or something, thinks L. Ray. Bad color.

"I need to ask you a few questions." Rhodes picks up several magazines and a yellow pad from the armless chair, sits down while glancing at the pad, lays them all on a table beside the chair, looks at the pad again, then at L. Ray. "About this movement you're starting."

So that's it. "Mr. Rhodes—may I call you Clarence?" L. Ray rolls his chair a couple of feet forward, his eyes on Rhodes, now seated across the room.

"Certainly."

"How old are you, Clarence, if I may ask?"

Clarence pauses. What the heck is going on here? he thinks. "Fifty-nine. But I—"

"I'm sixty-two. I can answer your questions, I think, with a brief overview: I've had four open-heart surgeries and suffer from fatigue sometimes. So I'm at a place in this old world where my life has caught up with me, and the other day I had a vision from God, through two Rose-haven ladies, that will bring to fruition Jesus' command-ment to care for the wretched of the world. I aim to start a volunteer movement to turn all nursing homes into churches and all churches into nursing homes. That's it. That's the show. What will come after that—given the potential spirit of love and concern created among strangers and people of all ages and religions—will be no telling what."

" 'People of all religions'? Mr. Flowers, America is in danger. Danger from within. You no doubt know that. We're starting a new millennium with Christianity more watered-down than at any time in history. Watered down by Americans. We can't afford watered-down Christianity. And frankly, I've gotten some complaints."

"About . . . ?"

"About your movement, religion, whatever it is, and that's why I'm here. I'll be frank." Clarence leans forward, drops an elbow to his knee. "I'm not a philosopher or theologian. I don't read books except for the Bible and Tom Clancy. So my point is, I want to know exactly what's going on."

"Let me say it in a different way, Clarence. This all started a while back when I was fishing out on McGarren Island and . . ."

OUT ON THE PORCH, in her wheelchair with her back against the wall, sits Darla Avery. She has seen the owner of the place go into L. Ray's room. He must be a friend. L. Ray is Mr. Connections; he can win over the devil—until he shows his hand.

Mr. Albright, her teacher, had been standing at the library door greeting students. She and L. Ray got in line behind a few couples. They had to show the tickets handed out in school that day.

In the big library room, a book smell held on above the punch and cookie and balloon and crepe paper smell. There was a record player, operated the whole time by Paul Douglas, who was also in shop. Paul was certified retarded.

Darla could dance like a fool—Glenda had taught her —and so could L. Ray, so that's exactly what they did. They danced just about every dance, bebopping. People would stop dancing and stand to watch them. Dancing turned her on. Like nothing else. When she did it real hard, she could pick up a leg and twist and turn and bend in a way that felt like little lightning bolts of gold. And the way L. Ray moved when he was dancing made her hungry for love, even at her age, or maybe especially at her age.

That's how it was—people dancing, and she and L. Ray dancing like fools, sweating their heads off—and she was having one of the best times of her life. They danced and drank punch and danced and drank punch and ate cookies and potato chips, and more than once, people stood and watched them dance all over the place, all that gold lightning zipping through her, and she was thinking to herself, This is what my life in high school is going to be like. Boys would watch her dance and would be asking her to football games and dances all the way through high school, and she'd be a cheerleader and pop-ular and very happy.

Parents came to pick up their children, sticking their heads in the library to look for their son or daughter, or stepping inside for a minute or two to watch and wait.

She and L. Ray were among the last to leave. They walked down that long wood-floored hall and out the door. She remembered that door, how heavy it was, the clanky handles. On this night, L. Ray held it open for her.

"Boy, that was fun, fun, fun," he said. "Want to go out to the Club Oasis for a little while?"

"Sure." She was game for just about anything.

They stopped at the Blue Light, and inside, L. Ray bought two tall Busches, then brought them out to the car in a paper bag. "Reach in that glove compartment and get me that church key," he said. He opened each beer with a swoosh, and then punched a little hole at the other side of the can top. "Drink up, Darla. Here's to a long and happy life." They clunked their beer cans together and she took a swallow. It was cold and it helped her move right on toward the top of the world, where she knew she was headed. Then he pushed in the lighter, and since he was driving, she lit them both a cigarette. She was in the boat of her life heading down the River of Heightened and Met Desires.

Inside the Club Oasis she didn't know too many of the girls, because for one thing they were all older. But she and L. Ray danced and danced and danced and sweated and sweated and sweated and went outside and smoked a cigarette, and Darla thought L. Ray might try to kiss her, but he didn't, and then they showed the stamps on their hands and went back inside.

• • •

DOWN IN 202, Clarence makes himself listen to Flowers.

"Like the entertainment we're fed these days," continues Flowers. "I'm sure you'll agree it's sick. Right?"

"Yes." The man can talk, thinks Clarence.

"Very sick. Well, I'm starting with old people. And I'm—"

"Okay. I have no problems with that, but what you're doing can be better handled at Mount Gilead Baptist Church, or Bethel Baptist, or any number of fine Southern Baptist churches we have in Hansen County."

"My movement is not unlike America. It's—"

"America was founded by Christians, Mr. Flowers. It's never needed more than that, and that's what it needs now. It's a Christian nation, under God, indivisible. It doesn't need—"

"I intend to do all I can to make Jesus proud. And this nation, by the way, was founded by men who were not Christians, exactly. I can't remember what they were— something. And 'under God' was stuck in there in the fifties, in the McCarthy era."

Clarence rises to leave. He knows it's the exact right moment. "This is not a threat, of course, but you need to know," he says, looking around the room—for what, he isn't sure— "that I own this establishment, and if my residents feel in any way threatened or insecure or afraid, or worried, then I'll have to do something about it, pronto.

So that's all I have to say right now. I just mainly want to get our conversation on record." He needs to move on.

"Thank you for stopping in."

Not as impressed upon as he ought to be, thinks Clarence.

"And pick up an apple there on your way out," says L. Ray. "They're Galas. I just discovered them. Got tired of the Delicious and decided to innovate."

Back in Anna's office, Clarence tells her, "When he gets his leg straightened out, Mr. Flowers needs to go."

O Brother

CARL PULLS HIS TAURUS into a spot in the parking lot of Meadow Hill Gardens. It looks like Anna lives in a corner town house. As he climbs the brick steps, he notices that they have separated an inch or so from the wooden porch. He rings the doorbell and concentrates on relaxing his vocal cords. "Hello, Anna," he practices in his lowest voice. "Hi there, Anna. What's up?"

The door opens. She is dressed in a plain black dress. A little girl with clear brown eyes holds to her leg and looks up at him.

"Hey, Anna," he says, his voice back up.

"Come in, Carl."

He steps up into the house, looks straight ahead—eyes level—at Anna's mouth, then up into her eyes.

Anna steps back. "This is Ruth."

"Hey," says Carl.

Ruth moves behind her mother.

Carl looks around; he hadn't known what to expect. The place looks comfortable and nice. If he'd been asked to picture where she lived, this would have been it.

"Have a seat," says Anna. "I'm in back with the sitter. I'll be right out." As she turns, Carl looks at the heels of her shoes. They are flat. He'd been hoping for heels.

He checks the words inked into the palm of his left hand as he sits down in a big, comfortable chair: *flowers, children, kidney infections, your job, Mr. Rhodes.* He doesn't want to end up in the middle of long silences. The chances are lower, he figures, with Anna. She has energy and force, and character. Or seems to. In his mind he rehearses asking, What do you think about Mr. Flowers?

He looks up. Ruth is sitting in a chair across the way, staring at him. Anna and the sitter are talking in a back room. What can he say to Ruth? He looks in his hand. Nothing there. "And your name is Ruth?"

"Yes."

She doesn't say, Yes sir. Who does anymore? "That's a pretty name."

"My mama has a boyfriend."

"Oh, is that right?"

"Yes. And he's a policeman."

"Oh. Is that right?"

"He's got a gun, too."

"That's good to know." What the . . . ? Was she joking?

Ruth says nothing. She slides from her seat and starts toward the back bedroom.

"I hope he doesn't shoot me," says Carl. He is thinking she might laugh, but she doesn't; he guesses she's too young. A policeman? Was that true?

Anna and the sitter are coming down the hall. He stands. Ruth has joined them.

"What are you two talking about?" Anna asks Ruth.

Ruth says nothing.

"I was just asking her name," says Carl.

"Mama, he's short."

"Sweetie, no, he's not. And what if he is?"

Oh boy, thinks Carl.

"Carl," says Anna, "this is Jennifer, our sitter. I'd introduce you to Lauren, but she's just about asleep. She's not feeling very well."

"How do you do?" Carl steps forward, extending his hand. Jennifer steps backward and holds out a limp hand.

"You've got the cell number," Anna says to Jennifer, "and Ruth, Jennifer has some dessert for you in the kitchen. And remember, bedtime is at eight-thirty." She turns with a smile to Carl. "Ready?"

"Let's hit the road," says Carl. He relaxes his vocal cords, but too late. If he says something now, it will sound funny.

• • •

HE IS HAPPY to see *O Brother* again, and afterward at the Slam Dunk Sports Bar, he sits with a 7UP on ice in front of him. Anna drinks from a glass of Diet Coke. He thought about drinking a beer, just to show her he can and will, but she ordered first, and he decided to play it safe. He doesn't want to offend her in any way. A small bowl of bar mix sits between them. They talk about the movie for a while. She doesn't seem to have liked it as much as he did, but she does ask him questions about the music, about Ralph Stanley and the Whites. He's seen them perform live. There is a period of silence. Ball games are on the four TV screens. She smiles.

He leans back just a bit and looks at his hand. He decides he'll do the best and most important thing first: ask about the policeman. Ruth probably made that up. "Ruth says you date a policeman?"

"Oh, she tells everybody that."

"Do you?"

"Date a policeman?"

"No. Do you brush your teeth every night?"

"What?"

"Just a joke." She sure missed that one. "Do you date a policeman?"

"It's an off-and-on kind of thing."

He nods, feeling something like dread. "So now I guess it's kind of off . . . or is it?"

"It is, and I don't know, I just . . . It's difficult. He's recently divorced, himself, and has a couple of kids.

It's very difficult to raise kids by yourself. That doesn't mean . . . I mean, marriage is not something I'm thinking about this soon after being divorced." She has on more eye makeup than she wears to work. That's a good thing, he figures. She's trying to look especially good—sexy, maybe.

"But I mean," she continues, "there's the whole money, or security, question, actually, but then too, even though my husband didn't spend an awful lot of time with the kids, an hour a day makes a difference. That adds up."

"Yep. That's thirty hours a week."

"A month, you mean."

"Yes, a month." What the hell am I doing? "I meant a month. About thirty hours a month . . . one a day." Damn. Silence. "Can be thirty-one, some months," says Carl. "Twenty-eight in—"

"February." Anna smiles and looks around.

He leans back slightly, looks at his hand.

"You're not dating anyone?" Anna asks.

Carl snaps his eyes up, bends to take a sip of 7UP. The clear plastic straw sticks in his nose. As he jerks his head up, it stays there. He grabs it.

She puts her hand over her mouth. Her eyes sparkle.

"Damn," he says. "Stabbed by a straw." He can't help laughing either. "Oh, no. I'm not dating anybody. Not exactly. Not now." He shouldn't have asked about the policeman. Big mistake. Not this early anyway.

" 'Not exactly'?" she says.

"Well, actually, no. I'm not dating anyone."

"What did you mean, 'not exactly'?"

"Well, what I meant is . . . what I wanted . . . I didn't want to seem like a . . . a loser." Yes. Tell her the truth.

"Anybody who takes as good care of an aunt as you do can't be a loser."

"She's always been my favorite aunt. Always made time for me. I think she had kind of a hard time with her husband. He was an alcoholic, and I think maybe abusive, though I don't know that he ever hit her."

"There are lots of ways to be abusive."

"Yes, I guess so."

"Did she have children?"

"No. None, except for me, in a way. She always gave me nice presents, took me places, let me drive her car. There weren't many children on her side of the family — on my father's side either, actually."

"What was he like?"

"My father?"

"No. Your hairstylist."

"Aha."

She is smiling.

A waiter sets a new bowl of bar mix on the table, takes away the empty bowl. Carl picks up some mix. "He was a good father. Kind of quiet. What about your folks?"

"It's just a plain family, except I'm close to my parents.

They've always been staunch Democrats, liberals—which is why I try to keep them up in Virginia. They might slow my career down here, with Mr. Rhodes at the helm and all."

"He's not a bad boss, is he?"

"Oh, no. Not at all. I know exactly what he expects."

Carl tries to picture what is written in his hand. "How old is that woman that sits on the porch across from Mrs. Talbert? She looks kind of young—compared."

"She is kind of young. Late fifties. She's very sick and is just getting her voice back after an esophagus infection that they thought they couldn't cure because of her immune-system deficiency. She's also got . . . well, let's just say she's pretty sick."

"Have you heard Miss Clara—what's her last name? —curse?" he asks. He suddenly realizes his voice is way up there. Now he'll have to lower it a little at a time, so there won't be a sudden drop.

"Mrs. Cochran? Oh, yes. Definitely. When I leave to go home, and she's on the porch, she says, 'I know you're tired. My ass is dragging too.' There are some funny things that go on out on that porch. The other day they were all out there, and Mrs. Lowe's great-niece, or great-great-niece, I guess it was, did a tap dance with a little tutu on and a tape deck playing music, and when it was over, they all clapped and Mrs. Talbert said, 'That's the best dancing I ever seen at a funeral.'"

Carl laughed. "Oh, man." He checks his hand again. "What do you think about Preacher Flowers?"

Anna takes a swallow of her Diet Coke. "Well, I know the progress on his leg has slowed considerably. It suddenly got stiff, he *says,* but he seems to be having the time of his life on the porch with some of the ladies, so I think there may be some faking going on there. I think he might not want to leave."

"That's what I was thinking."

"Except Mrs. Lowe and her niece, Emily, came in to complain about some kind of movement he's trying to get started, and Mr. Rhodes is on his high horse about that. You sort of like him—Mr. Flowers—don't you?"

"Well, at first I didn't. I thought he was a kind of crackpot, which I still think he might be, but I've been wanting to play an electric bass for a long time, and he more or less dropped one in my lap."

"You all sound good together."

"Yeah, I kind of enjoyed that the other night." Voice back up—get it down.

"He's not as strange as his niece; I know that. Actually, I shouldn't be talking out of shop, but she's one pretty strange woman."

Anna's cell phone rings. "I'm sorry," she says. "Hello? . . . Yes. . . . How much? . . . A hundred and three?" She looks at Carl. "We'll be right there." She snaps the phone cover shut. "I'm sorry. Lauren has a fever. It's probably an ear infection. I was afraid of this. She wasn't feeling well this afternoon."

"No problem. Well, I mean it's a problem, but I understand." Carl feels sorry to leave, but the pressure to make conversation has lifted.

They head for Meadow Hill Gardens, where he has no chance for anything beyond a brief good-bye.

Shopping for High Heels

IT'S THE BIGGEST RABBIT Lil has ever seen. She and Clara wait in the lobby, all dressed up, sitting in wing chairs on each side of the large ceramic rabbit near the gas fireplace. They are waiting for Carl to take them shopping.

"That's the biggest rabbit I've ever seen," says Lil. She is dressed in her favorite sweat suit, the pink one, a green scarf, a green windbreaker, and brown loafers. "They ought to have another one in here to keep that one company."

"I think it's kind of stupid-looking," says Clara. "So big. They ought to have some big ceramic hound dogs in here." Clara wears tan Hush Puppies, green pants, and a blue jacket with green flowers on it.

An alarm sounds at the automatic doors. Lil knows who it is before she looks. Mr. Grayson—too close to the door. There he stands in that brown button-up sweater that hangs down to his butt. He is always waving imaginary butterflies away from his eyes—because of lead poisoning—and he isn't allowed outside, so he has this little radio, or sensor or something, around his neck that sets off a door alarm if he gets too close. Lil has asked Anna about the lead poisoning, and she says it's from a factory job up north. He never has any visitors.

Anna, returning from somewhere down the hall, stops and talks softly to Mr. Grayson, steering him away from the doors just as Lil sees Mr. Rhodes come in.

"Ladies," says Mr. Rhodes. "So good to see you."

"Mr. Rhodes?" Clara squints with her good eye. "What the hell's happened to the corn bread around here?"

Lil notices him glancing at Clara's name tag.

"I don't know, Mrs. Cochran. But I'll do my best to find out. What exactly is the problem with the corn bread?"

"The taste."

"How so? Help me out." He smiles.

"It don't have much taste and it's too crumbly. It falls apart." That's what Lil likes about Clara. She says what she thinks. Beatrice and Maudie can't stand her cursing, and Lil pretends to be bothered by it, but she secretly doesn't mind at all. It brightens the dullness of this . . . this life after life.

"I'll get on that, Mrs. Cochran, and I'll bet you it's better next time I see you. I'll be asking you about it."

"My nephew is coming to take us shopping," says Lil.

"Oh, that's nice."

"His name is Carl. You met him. Right out there on the porch. He just got promoted not all that long ago and he's the best thing to me. I don't know what I'd do without him."

"Oh, yes. Fine young man."

He's thinking about something else, thinks Lil.

Carl, coming through the front door, sees Mr. Rhodes talking to his aunt and Mrs. Cochran and decides to drop in on Anna for a minute.

Anna's office door is open. A man (a resident's family member?) is sitting across from her desk, talking with her. Anna smiles at Carl, holds up a finger, signaling for him to wait one minute. Carl feels a rush of delight—she seems glad to see him.

He waits in the hall. She follows her visitor out her door, stops one step closer to Carl than he thinks normal. He looks up into her face and stands as tall as he can.

She steps back toward her office. "Come in and have a seat."

As she turns, he looks at the heels of her shoes. They are flat. That's not going to change, he thinks. He relaxes his vocal cords, coughs at the lowest pitch he can manage.

Carl sits, and Anna sits in the soft chair beside her

desk. He's only seen her sit there while he's in her office. Maybe that means something good, though he can't say exactly what. "I'm about to take Aunt Lil and Mrs. Cochran shopping. Do you want to come?"

"I'd love to, but I'm afraid I can't."

The word *love* holds on for a few seconds. "It should be a pretty exciting trip," he says. "They want to buy some shoes."

"That could be a prolonged process." She has that way of slightly tilting her head.

"That's what I'm afraid of." Carl is suddenly conscious of what he's wearing. Plaids are probably not in style anymore. He should have worn his solid white dress shirt, open at the collar. Like that picture of George Clooney.

There are two sharp knocks on the open door, and Mr. Rhodes walks into the office. "Hello, Anna. And you are. . . . ?" Mr. Rhodes extends his hand.

"Carl Turnage." Big, strong hand.

"Oh, yes, your aunt was just telling me about you. I've seen you around. She's very thankful for all your help. And she looks good." He sits down in the remaining chair, seems relaxed and comfortable to Carl, like he's in a place where he can be himself, where he might even tell a joke, laugh a bit. "By the way, Carl," he says, "do you know Mr. Flowers—L. Ray?"

"I've talked to him out on the porch."

"Do you know anything about a movement—or cult—he's trying to start?"

"No, not really. I don't know anything about it. I think he . . . I've just heard him talk about normal preacher things."

"Well, we don't want any trouble here that will upset the ladies."

CARL DRIVES HIS TAURUS. Aunt Lil sits up front with him, and Mrs. Cochran sits in back behind Aunt Lil. As they pull out onto Langston Avenue, Aunt Lil turns and says loudly, "Don't you wish you had a nephew that would do for you the way this one does for me?"

"I got two nephews," says Mrs. Cochran. "They both *work*."

Yeah, well, Carl thinks, bless your pointy little head. "I work," he says. "I've just had a pretty flexible schedule in the last year or two. Some good people working for me. They know how to keep things going, you know?" He looks into the rearview mirror, sees the glaring glass eye behind the lens.

At Crosspoints Mall's upper east entrance, Carl stops the car, gets out, and opens the back door to get the walkers. Aunt Lil's billfold drops out of her saddlebag onto the asphalt. Carl picks it up and puts it back in the bag. Her saddlebag is navy blue. Mrs. Cochran's is tan. As Carl parks the car, they stand in their walkers by the front door.

In Penney's, the two ladies stop every few tables to look at items.

Carl moves on a few steps. "Let's find the shoes. You all wanted to buy some shoes." He waits. "You said you wanted to—"

"I need shoes," says Mrs. Cochran.

"Well, let's find the shoes."

Carl's men are installing aluminum awnings at the alumni house at Ballard College, and he needs to get by and check on them as soon as he can. He asks a saleslady where the shoes are. She says downstairs and points toward an escalator. He looks. How can . . . how can he get them down that safely?

At the escalator, he gives instructions: They are to wait up top. He'll fold the walkers and take them down, then come back up and escort the ladies to the bottom, one at a time.

When Carl is about halfway down, Lil says to Clara, "Why are we waiting up here?"

"Beats me. You just step on a step. But you step on a crack and you bust your ass."

Carl heads back up. He looks over at the down escalator and . . . and there they are, Aunt Lil and then Mrs. Cochran, floating down, their eyes locked straight ahead. He imagines Aunt Lil hitting bottom, never lifting her feet, and Mrs. Cochran tumbling over her. He turns to run back down, but there are too many people.

Up top, he looks down; they aren't there. Good news, maybe. He heads down and finds them standing in their walkers—in menswear. Mrs. Cochran is examining neckties.

"You all were supposed to wait for me."

Aunt Lil looks at him sharply. "What?"

"You all were—"

"Are those Cheerios painted on this tie?" Mrs. Cochran holds up a tie.

"You all were supposed to wait up top for me. I didn't want you coming down by yourselves. No, I think they're boat steering wheels."

Mrs. Cochran looks at Carl through her thick glasses, over her bird-beak nose, her big glass eye not moving, a frown on her face, and says, "We were fine. Don't they have elevators?"

Carl feels a little dense. Of course. "I didn't think about that, but it doesn't look like we need one, does it?"

"I don't use elevators as a matter of principle," says Aunt Lil.

"Then why'd you use the escalator?" Mrs. Cochran asks.

"Because they don't have stairs anymore, do they? It's like everything else: in with the complicated, out with the simple."

"You can say that again."

In the shoe department, Carl sits down while the ladies look at shoes just behind him.

"They all look so new," says Mrs. Cochran.

"I hope so," says Aunt Lil.

"I always liked a high heel. What do you think, Carl?"

Carl shrugs. "I don't know."

A few minutes later, he hears Mrs. Cochran say, "Help in a store these days is scarce as tits on a boar hog. I'll just . . . sit down and put these on myself." She rolls her walker around near Carl. The shoes are in her saddlebag. "I think they're just my size. Let me get my glasses," she says, still standing. This takes a few minutes. "Yep. Seven and a half. Just my size." She slowly situates herself and sits down. So does Aunt Lil.

Carl pulls up a salesperson's stool, sits, gets the new shoe on Mrs. Cochran's right foot, helps her push her heel down into it. She smells like talcum powder and lavender.

She starts to stand up, sits back.

"Don't you want to put both of them on?" Carl asks her. "No."

"You probably need to get you some shoes with flat bottoms. It's easy to turn your ankle in high heels."

She starts to stand, sits again, then gives another push and stands. She starts out in her walker. She goes *up* on the high heel, down on the flat. *Up* on the high heel, down on the flat.

"I think you need flat bottoms." Carl wishes Anna could see this. He looks around. "How about some of those white slip-ons?"

A clerk appears, and for another twenty minutes the ladies try on shoes, with the clerk going back into the stacks four or five times, and finally both Lil and Mrs. Cochran decide on white canvas slip-ons. They pay with their MasterCards.

Outside, Carl discovers a soft drizzle and the smell of hot asphalt, freshly wet. Lil and Mrs. Cochran wait under the sheltered lower east entrance while he gets the car.

L. Ray works on a sermon out on the porch. He looks up—to listen to Mrs. Lowe and Mrs. Satterwhite, who are sitting nearby. Mrs. Lowe is complaining about somebody stealing a comb from her dresser top.

The sermon is about the name of his new movement, but he's gotten nowhere. *The name will come, just as rain will come. Think about naming rain. It finally gets called the best thing you can ever call it. Rain.*

Darla Avery holds her eyes on the back of L. Ray's head as he writes. The two ladies over there stand to go in because of the rain. L. Ray rolls back away from the porch railing.

Darla will stay where she is. She's dry.

She and L. Ray left the Club Oasis at about eleven. When she got in the front seat with him this time, she moved a little ways away from the passenger door, toward him. He didn't say anything at all as they left, which seemed odd, and he had driven less than a mile when he turned onto a side road, drove a half mile or so, pulled over on the shoulder, cut the ignition. She thought to herself, This is where we neck. She was nervous, wondering what it would be like, wondering if a car might drive by.

And this is where it gets almost too embarrassing to *think* about.

No sooner was his hand off the car keys than he said, of all things, "Darla, have you ever seen a man's pecker?"

She was shocked. She couldn't help picturing her brothers and daddy when they went swimming in the Vickers' pond. "Yes."

"Well, let me tell you what I'm going to have to do. I'm going to have to take mine out and give it a beating. He's been a naughty boy."

What could she do? She felt like she was locked in a casket, and she got scared.

He sat right there under the steering wheel, unzipped his pants, and pulled out his thing. She looked out the window, but it was like looking into a mirror: the window reflected everything in the eerie green light of the dashboard.

"Oh, blessed Jesus," he said right before he started masturbating, and she just looked out the window at the night. Her mind was blank, everything suspended-like, and suddenly there were headlights coming from behind them. A car whizzed by, but he kept at it: "Oh, blessed Jesus, would you look at me, Darla? Would you look at me?"

She couldn't help seeing his reflection. He threw his head back and started his hand going faster and . . . her insides collapsed, her heart and her hopes. What was happening might as well have been physical for the hurt, the dirty and completely useless and invisible way it made her feel. She tried to look out the window, and he said, "Look, look, look," and she said, "I can see you in the reflection, L. Ray. I'm not going to look at you. You take me home right now." And he said, "*Arrrrrrrrr*. Hallelujah!" Then he opened his door, the inside light came on, and he slung his hand toward the ground.

He needed to be castrated—still needs it. There's no telling how many times he's done something like that, or worse. Maybe even far worse. Ruined people, girls, no telling how young.

"L. Ray, you take me home now," she'd said, "or I'm going to tell Mr. Albright."

"Okay." As cool and calm as he could be. "Let me clean up a little here. Are you sure?"

"Yes!"

He got out his handkerchief. And in no time they were driving home. Total silence. She could feel her face and neck were red as a beet. He walked her to her door, said good night, and was gone. She would not look at him. Inside, on the table beside the couch, was the box and

the green paper and white bow. The flap-and-snap billfold was in her pocketbook. She sat down on the couch
and realized her legs were shaky. And then she started
crying.

L. RAY WRITES, occasionally glancing out at the
drizzle. *We must start the effort of saving and salving
down the whole green-and-brown ball, Earth, with some
kind of awareness of suffering, some kind of balm, some
kind of felt need to relieve the suffering of our old people.
We can start it right here at Rosehaven. Within our neon-
damaged culture, the act of relieving suffering, that com-
mitment, can have real power to show up the greedy for
what they are—and it's the only thing that can do it.
Each of us, separately, with eyes averted from our own or
others' suffering, individual beating hearts, each beat
thumping a slight hunger for a little peace and quiet in the
immensity of this wide universe's galaxies of fire and vast
vacancies of whisper-yawning space—each of us needs
help. Praise the God in us all as we heal ourselves by
tending to the noble old in those ways we would have
ourselves tended to. We are about this, ladies: We are
about a change in the world. We want to make the world
of winter into a world of spring.*

He tries to remember where he was that winter afternoon when he looked out of his motel window at the
shopping center under construction across the street. Was

it Philadelphia or Pittsburgh? The bare, drab earth scraped of all green, the weather miserable, the big building under construction with some kind of yellow siding that had large print on it, the telephone wires between him and the construction—like a sad photograph, all of it worked on him while he decided what to do with the rest of his life, whether to go home or go to the family of the woman who had died while he was trying to heal her, while he was doing his best to physically, with his hands, infuse the healing spirit of God into her bones and heart and brain, back when he believed that could be done. Well, hell, it could be done—he'd done it. But he sure didn't understand it. He'd also faked it. On occasion.

So he had decided to start over, to change his name and start over, and soon after that came the shark attack, and now here he is in a damn nursing home, but with a hope in something big—something he can do. If he doesn't make a difference *now*—if this movement doesn't get launched—then that's all she wrote. But by God, he's found a slant that is fresh and powerful, a slant of all slants, handed to him by two old ladies, and he's going to launch this thing, even though he can't think or hear or see so well all the time. But part of a visionary's, a prophet's, job is to get people to behave in ways that will lead to the well-being of everyone. He can do that. The Bible prophets were mostly old people, old folks, geezers, seniors, silvers. None of those words sound bad or odd to him, now that he's one of them himself and doing something worth a dime. He's proud of his age. He's by God sick of the big American marketing frenzy ignoring and thus belittling old people. And in the process of his movement, whenever it comes, the world's tension level will drop by 10 or 20 percent, and that will set the stage for a time of new help for old people, of saving the silvers, bailing out the baldies, giving help where it is needed, for heaven's sake, instead of craving candy, coveting cars, and wasting gasoline. He doesn't have to worry too much about the details. Jesus didn't—and look at what he launched. With a new slant. Jesus didn't have a secretary either. But he did have disciples. They will come with time. Give it a little time. Get it launched, and then give it a little time. This bass player, that Carl fellow, can be a disciple.

He looks up, and here comes Carl along the walkway, behind Clara Cochran and Lil Olive, holding one umbrella over them as they push their walkers along, and another umbrella over his own head. Their walker satchels are stuffed with white shopping bags.

"You all been shopping?" asks L. Ray.

Carl is shaking off the umbrellas.

Clara brushes water off her sleeve. "That's right. Got us some shoes. I need to get in and get some rest. My ass is dragging."

"Clara!" says Lil.

L. Ray thinks again about Carl—a levelheaded young

man. Carl might be the one to put his new sermons about the movement in a book, just in case L. Ray doesn't last long enough. The fellow seems competent and doesn't seem to have any of his own eggs to fry. Except he likes Anna. And who doesn't.

DARLA WATCHES THEM ALL. As the woman with the big eye walks past her, Darla decides that she's the right one to tell first. "He masturbated in front of me."

The woman stops. "What?"

"He masturbated in front of me."

Clara has never really looked into those eyes—eyes with dark bags beneath them. "Who?"

"L. Ray Flowers."

"Aw, bullshit. Sober up."

Darla can't believe it. This must be one of the crazy ones. "You get on inside where you belong, old woman. You old bitch. I know what happened."

"You ought to be ashamed of yourself."

"Well, I'm not. I didn't do anything wrong. He's the one that did the wrong. You get away from me."

That night back then, her mama and daddy weren't home yet, and her little sister, Melanie, came in and said, "Where have you been?" Melanie was in her pajamas. She was seven then. They were soft pajamas, flannel, yellow with white ducks; they had been Darla's when she was little. Melanie was wearing her glasses. She was farsighted.

"Where's Mama and Daddy?" Darla asked her.

"They went to the drive-in."

"Why didn't you go?"

"They said I couldn't. Where have you been?"

"To a dance."

"Who did you go with?"

"A boy I know."

"Who?"

"Just a boy."

"Was it fun?"

"Yes." That was her first lie about it, and then she didn't say anything for, what, more than forty years? She'd been ashamed of it.

"Then why are you crying?" her sister had said. She jumped up on the couch beside Darla, crossed her legs, and grabbed her toes.

"I'm crying because I'm happy."

Melanie looked at the wrapping paper. "What did you get for a present?"

"A billfold."

"Can I have that bow?"

Darla focuses. Here comes another crazy one, with her nephew. Who should she tell now? The social worker? The owner? She starts rolling in, and the nephew holds the door for her.

She still has the billfold. That night was supposed to be the first big night of her life.

L. Ray is still on the porch when his bass player, Carl, comes back out.

"You writing a song?" asks Carl.

"A sermon. I'm on a roll. Sit down."

"I've just got a minute." Carl looks at his watch.

He's in a hurry, thinks L. Ray. But I can hook him. "I'm trying to give some credits. I was just thinking that my whole shark rebirth couldn't have happened if I hadn't read a book called *Who Wrote the Bible?* You haven't read that, by chance, have you?"

"Nope. I think the last book reading I did was back in the eighth grade or somewhere in there. We had a paperback reading club. There was, let's see, *The Red Car* and *The Kid Comes Back,* and . . . Did you ever read either one of those?"

"Can't say as I did. But this *Who Wrote the Bible?* had a kind of transforming effect on me, along with some other transformations. It says a lot about the Bible and it's convincing and it just gets me to thinking in ways that . . . You might not be interested."

"I got about all the church I could handle when I was growing up."

"Yeah, but the old hymns stay with you, don't they?"

"I guess—yes, they do."

"I think we ought to work up some. I'm going to do another little sermon Thursday night. I've written seven." L. Ray is thinking that an advance man doesn't have to believe anything. This fellow can be his advance man. Just somebody to set things up so he can come in and mow 'em down, rev 'em up, get some excitement going. "I used to be on the road, like I told you, back in the Midwest for a while, until I had some misfortune come along."

"What happened?"

"Just an accident. I don't like to think about it. I went through a pretty bad spell. There were several months I didn't have anything much to eat. A lot of beans." The accident, L. Ray thinks, was an accident, and that's it. Nobody seems to realize that or believe that or something. It could have happened in a supermarket, on the street, anywhere. It was an accident. Accidents are part of life.

"Speaking of beans," says Carl, "I took one of my workers home sick last week and went in with him, and he asked me to get him something out of the refrigerator. He had a six-pack of Budweiser in there, two packs of baloney, and a pound of bacon. That was it."

"There's another song for you."

Thunder Road

MRS. CELIA ROGERS parks her car in the front parking lot at Rosehaven, near the porch. She drove from Greensboro to see her sister, Jenny Osborne, and because she's afraid she might lose her keys inside that big building, or somewhere else—she's losing and forgetting stuff left and right these days—she leaves her keys right there where she'll remember. In the ignition. It's an '89 Olds. Maroon. Luggage rack on the trunk.

FROM THE PORCH, Lil can see the luggage rack on her car trunk, right there in the front parking lot, and she sees no reason to sit on the porch when she can ride in her car, even do a little shopping maybe. Carl hasn't told her she can't—yet. Her friends are right there beside her on the porch. She leans forward in her rocking chair and asks, "Do you all want to go for a little ride?"

"We can't do that," says Clara.

"My car is right there, and I have a driver's license, for goodness' sakes."

"Oh."

"Let me go get my pocketbook," says little Maudie.

"You won't need it. I got mine." Lil picks it up from beside her chair. "Let's see, where are my keys?"

"I might need it. I'll be right back."

"I wonder if Carl left the keys in there. He drove it last."

SOMEHOW THIS DOES not feel quite like—drive like—her car. That Carl did something to it. She turns left onto one of the widest highways she has ever seen. "When in the world did they put this here?" she asks.

Clara is up front with Lil. Beatrice and Maudie are in back.

"It's been here ever since they built it," says Clara. "Don't drift over to the middle like that."

"I don't even recognize where I am anymore," says Maudie.

"They've built so many goddamned new buildings," says Clara.

Beatrice leans forward. "I wish you wouldn't use that language. It's unbecoming."

They ride awhile in silence. Lil remembers driving to the beach alone after Tad got so he couldn't go. She thinks about the earlier time he went to the beach alone and stayed two weeks and she didn't tell anybody, not even her sisters. That wasn't long after that boy showed up. Should she tell Carl about all that? She pictures her torn-up marriage certificate.

"Lil, that light is red," says Clara.

"What light?"

"That stoplight hanging up . . . Lil! You just ran that red light!"

"I never saw a red light."

"My goodness. You're going to kill us all."

"I feel like I'm already dead most of the time," says Beatrice.

Lil wonders if Clara is just seeing things.

"They *have* built a lot of new buildings," says Maudie. "It seems like there are more buildings than there are companies."

Beatrice, still getting settled, pulls at her slip through her skirt. "That's because they've got more than one company in a building."

Lil is thinking, Now, this one doesn't have a clutch, does it? She leans back, tries to look into the floorboard. Maybe there *was* a red light. "Well, there wasn't anybody coming, was there?"

"I don't guess so," says Clara, "else they'd be in here

with us." She looks over her shoulder. "Maudie, if they had more than one company in a building, then there would be more companies than buildings, not more buildings than companies."

"What did I say?"

What in the world are they talking about? thinks Lil. Where am I?

"You said there are more—Lil! There's another red light. Damn! Stop!"

Lil sees it, hits the brake. Whoops! The brakes are sensitive. Tires screech. The car slides to a stop. Carl has had the brakes worked on. People crossing the street stare, draw back a little. Well, she thinks, at least my reflexes are still all right. She'd been looking for stoplights over there on a telephone pole on the corner, not hanging overhead. That's all.

Clara leans toward Lil, stares at her with her one good eye. "Lil, can you by God see?"

"I certainly can. I just haven't driven in a while is all. I was looking in the wrong place for stoplights. I'm out of practice. Carl has this idea that he don't want me driving. You need to practice driving just like you need to practice anything else."

"How about the way Carl played that guitar?" Beatrice says from the backseat.

Lil looks in the rearview mirror. She can see Beatrice but not little Maudie. "He always has been musical but just never got off to a good start." Lil wonders what Carl will say about this driving. He won't like it. But it's her car, after all. It was good of him to tighten up those brakes.

"If you look in the yellow pages," says somebody— it's little Maudie—"you just have the names of companies listed, but if you drive along the street just about anywhere in Hansen County, certainly in Summerlin, there is building after building after building. Lil, you can go now. The light's green."

What can we shop for today? thinks Lil as she drives across the intersection. "Why don't we get something for Mr. Flowers's new idea?"

"Our idea," says Clara.

"That's right."

"That's a good idea," says Beatrice. "What?"

"Let's get him a flag," says Clara. "Every movement needs a flag."

Maudie straightens, pushes up in her seat a bit. We need to stay out of that business, she thinks. "He's going to get into trouble with all that. It's blasphemous, number one, and number two, it might be connected to those one-world-government black helicopter groups. The man is messing with the basics of Christianity, trying to get all the other religions in on it."

"Aw, Maudie," says Clara, "lighten up."

Lil is glad she said that.

"You mark my words."

Lil fails to recognize any familiar landmarks. "That Eckerd wasn't there before. The one I know is over at the intersection of Market and Dillard. Mr. Butler works there. He's the pharmacist. Cliff Butler. He's one of the best pharma—whoops!"

Clara grabs the dash. "Lil!? Holy smoke."

"One of the best pharmacists and nicest men you'll ever meet anywhere. Do any of you know him?"

"Oh, yes," says Maudie. "I been knowing him since he —slow down, Lil—since he started working over there. Before him was Mr. Bordeaux, and I think he was just as nice as Mr. Butler, myself."

Lil expects to come to Highway 98 right about now, but it's nowhere to be seen. "I thought Highway Ninety-eight was right along here. Everything has changed so much."

"Highway Ninety-eight is clear on the other side of town," says Clara. "You turned left out of Rosehaven, not right."

"Okay, then I need to turn around. How about right here?"

The car bounces into a strip-mall parking lot.

"Slow down, Lil. For crying out loud."

"I don't have a backseat driver. I got a front-seat driver." Lil looks over at Clara and smiles.

"Keep your eye on the road—on the parking lot!" says Clara. "Your eyes."

"I've got to tinkle," says Maudie.

"I could go myself," says Beatrice.

" 'Tinkle'?" says Clara. "There's a parking place."

Lil pulls in and stops the car. She's kind of glad to be safe. Maudie is already getting out from right behind her. With that three-pod cane, she's pretty fast, and she's already standing there as Lil opens her door.

"You're over the center line."

Lil looks, then looks back inside the car. Everybody is getting out. "They won't mind. We're not going to be gone that long. Unless they've got flags and we have to pick one out. That might take a while."

Maudie hands Lil her walker from the backseat floorboard as Beatrice and Clara get theirs. They start in single file for the CVS. Lil pulls up the rear, looks ahead to see who is in the lead: little Maudie. She and that three-pod cane are always out front.

Inside, they gather together, and Lil says, "Let's get some candy."

Maudie raises her cane slightly, pointing to the back. "I just want to go to the bathroom."

"I want me two big packs of midget Tootsie Rolls," says Lil. "What about you, Clara?"

Clara looks around. "I could use some M&M's."

Maudie heads for the back of the store. Beatrice follows.

Lil realizes that there probably won't be any flags in a

drugstore. "Where in the world do you buy flags?" she asks Clara.

"Beats me. I never heard of a flag store, but where the hell *do* all the flags come from?"

AT ROSEHAVEN, MAUDIE'S cousin Cathy Loggins has arrived for a visit. She looks in Maudie's room, on the porch, in the sunroom, the TV room, the library, and the chapel. Where can she be? She knocks on the social worker's door—Anna Guthrie, the nameplate says. The door is not quite closed.

"Yes?"

"Hi, I'm Cathy Loggins. My cousin is Maudie Lowe, the little short woman, and I can't seem to find her anywhere."

"Well, let's go looking," says the social worker as she stands. "I'm Anna Guthrie. How do you do?"

"Just fine."

On the porch, Anna leans over to a woman who is staring at Cathy's shoes, and asks loudly, "Mrs. Talbert, have you seen Maudie Lowe?"

Mrs. Talbert looks up. "She went shopping."

"Shopping? Who with?"

"There was seven or eight of them."

"I don't think that's possible."

Another woman rushes up to Anna. "Somebody has stolen my car!" she says.

"Oh, my goodness," says the social worker. "I'll call the sheriff. Come on, so we can give a description of your car. I'm so sorry."

MAUDIE DECIDES THAT since the others use walkers and she uses a cane, she should be more or less in charge. They are all standing in a group trying to decide what to do. There will be no flag business. The very idea.

She says she'll take the candy orders and get the candy while the others sit in the pharmacy waiting area, where there is a blood pressure machine. Beatrice promptly sits at the machine and sticks her arm through the hole. Maudie takes candy orders from Lil and Clara, goes to the candy aisle, finally finds the M&M's, and pulls a bag off the prong. Midget Tootsie Rolls next. They seem to be hidden. Plenty of regulars, but no midgets. She finally finds a bag hung behind a bag of regulars.

She makes her way back to the cash register, near the waiting area, looks all around, doesn't see the others. She looks down the aisles. There—they're all looking at something. She approaches. They are inspecting folding aluminum lawn chairs.

Clara sees her, turns, holds up a chair. "I've found a chair I want." It's green and gold. "Lil's going to let me use her MasterCard."

Maudie carries the chair—because she has a spare hand —back to the cash register, where they decide who owes what so they can pay Lil back. The salesperson writes it down for them. Nobody, not even the salesperson, can read the receipt.

As soon as they get outside, Clara turns to Maudie. "I want to carry my chair."

"I can carry it."

Clara stops and won't go anywhere until Maudie hands her the chair.

"It's so light," says Clara. "You know, if we saw the right color, we could buy one and make a flag out of it. That would make a pretty flag."

"We're not doing any flags today," says Maudie.

"Well, Maudie, I wouldn't count on it," says Clara. "In fact, if we were to vote, you'd lose."

Maudie stops, turns. The others are in a kind of gaggle behind her. Best not to respond, Maudie decides. That's just crazy talk. She turns to lead them toward the car. Where is that car?

Just as they all reach the curb, Clara, from behind her, says, "Oh, there's a Hardee's. Let's get a cheeseburger. I'm hungry."

"That's a good idea," says Lil. "I could use a cheeseburger myself."

"Where is Hardee's?" says Beatrice.

"Right there in front of you," says Clara. "Hell, I ain't got but one good eye and I can see that."

"Shouldn't we put that chair in the car, then?" Maudie asks Clara.

"Oh no, I want to take it into Hardee's and try it out, and if I don't like it, I can carry it back."

Maudie notices a big brown car, with a star on the side and red and blue lights up top, moving by slowly. The man inside—a sheriff?—is looking right at them as it passes. The brake lights brighten; the car stops, then pulls into a parking place.

DEPUTY HOLLIS, WHO has been up most of the night chasing drug dealers through the woods at the old Sapp place, stands in line at Hardee's, about to order for four ladies. He wears a black nylon-mesh ball cap because it lets in air. Sometimes he worries that people can see his bald head through the tiny holes. His eyes feel bloodshot and swollen. His radio broadcast the bulletin about the ladies just before he stopped at the drugstore to get some Tylenol. Wait'll the guys hear about this, he thinks.

He returns to their table. The one with a big eye is trying to unfold a lawn chair over her walker. "This way," she says, "if I don't like it, I can just carry it back." Her name tag says Clara something. They are *all* wearing name tags.

He puts their food down on the table. "Here, let me help." He unfolds Clara's chair for her and sets it partly in the aisle. All four of them ordered cheeseburgers, and two of them ordered fries. A Coke, a 7UP, and two Diet Cokes are in the corners of the cardboard tray. It is quarter past eleven in the morning and he has just eaten pork chops, tomatoes, and hash browns at Waffle House.

The one named Lil says, "I'm sure that car is mine." She is looking at him kind of hard.

"No ma'am, that car belongs to somebody else."

"I think it's mine. I think you're mistaken."

"No ma'am. Somebody left the keys in it at Rose-haven."

"Lil, you told us that was your car," says the big one.

"Well, I think it is. I wouldn't take somebody else's car, for heaven's sake. How did somebody get my keys in there? Three keys."

"The keys are . . . I don't think they are your keys, ma'am."

"What's the third key for?" asks the big one.

Hollis checks her name tag: Beatrice Satterwhite.

"My apartment."

"We can go see if it will open your apartment," says Beatrice.

"No ma'am. I got to get on down to the station and write up a report."

"They give you all homework?" asks Beatrice.

"No ma'am, just a report."

"Do we get to ride back in your police car?"

"Yes ma'am."

"Lord, they'll think we've been arrested," says Lil.

"I want to ask you something," says Beatrice to Hollis. "Can you maybe stop somewhere on the way back and let me shoot your gun?"

"No ma'am. I can't do that."

Beatrice remembers going grouse hunting with a group from her husband's company during Christmas vacation one year. The ladies were allowed to shoot. Somebody had put the birds out in a field, and they could drive a jeep right up to a bird after the dog pointed. She had refused to shoot, and her husband never let her forget it. She'd sworn to him that she'd shoot a gun the next time she got a chance. Then he died. And here is her chance. "Isn't there a shooting range or a field or something between here and Rosehaven?"

"No ma'am."

"Where'd you get your gun training?"

"We have a range."

"Why can't we stop by there?"

"I've got some other things I've got to be doing."

"Like what?" Beatrice takes a bite of her cheeseburger.

"I've got to write up my drug bust."

"We don't have any drugs!"

"No ma'am. That was before I got here."

Lil believes somebody has played a trick on her. Surely Carl somehow is behind this—to teach her some kind of lesson by bringing the sheriff in on everything.

Hollis notices that the one with the glass eye is eating very slowly. He thinks, How long does it take a ninety-year-old lady trying out a lawn chair to eat a cheeseburger?

"Did you know, Mr. Hollis," says the big one, "that the cannibals had a cannibal for their God?"

"No ma'am, I don't think I did."

"Mr. Flowers, a preacher at Rosehaven, told us that the other day while we were sitting out on the porch, and he says communists and capitalists are the same way. Isn't that an interesting thing? He's going to put it in a sermon."

"I don't think the communists are allowed to have a God."

"That's right. That's because their God is a communist. See how it all works out?"

"I think Mr. Flowers is dangerous," says the tiny one.

"I think he makes people happy with his music," says the car thief. "That's one thing. He's teaching my nephew," she says to Mr. Hollis, "how to play a guitar with just four strings."

The one with the eye looks over her drink cup, eyebrows furrowed. "I thought he already played."

"Oh no, he's always been a big music *listener*."

"So you all belong to the same nursing home, more or less?"

"That's right," says Maudie. "And I think this preacher man out there is a lunatic."

"Mr. Hollis," says the big one, "did you know that

Walter Cronkite gave me four thousand dollars, and that whore-hopping son of mine spent every cent of it in Reno, Nevada?"

"No ma'am," says Hollis. She is looking right at him —into his eyes, like he ought to be saying something. He is tired. He lifts his ball cap, wipes his head with his arm, replaces the cap. "No ma'am. I didn't."

"Well, he did, and now he's up and traveling all the way acrost the United States."

Hollis nods his head. He's not in much of a talking mood. "Let's hit the road, ladies. As soon as you finish that cheeseburger, ma'am."

A-1 Hair

CARL IS THINKING ABOUT ANNA. He'll stop by her office, say hello. He's at Rosehaven to take Aunt Lil to the Piccadilly—and also at some point to have a little heart-to-heart about her driving, find out exactly what happened. Anna called yesterday after the incident. And then they'll be off to buy a wig at A-1 Hair, still run by Aunt Lil's old business-school classmate, Emma Brown.

As Carl approaches Anna's office door, he thinks she's having a coughing fit, her head bent down and her hands over her mouth. Then he realizes she's crying. Behind the door but not out of sight is a gray pant leg with a black stripe down the side and a spit-polished shoe on a big foot. The policeman? Her . . . her boyfriend? He steps back. Maybe they are breaking up. Maybe the guy has just told her they have to break up, or maybe . . . maybe she's just told *him* they have to break up and is pretending to cry. He heads toward Aunt Lil's room. He thinks about those two little girls. He'd only seen the one, Ruth. Could he raise them? He probably shouldn't think about that, but he can't help it. Can he be a father? What would he do when he was alone with them? Take them places? On hikes? To movies? To a park somewhere? He could push them in swings. He knows how to do that. How big *is* this policeman? He pictures him losing his temper, pulling back his fist. Maybe he should just back off, wait for some signal from her. He thinks about the way she tilts her head, the shape of her face, her eyes, her big lips . . . but he doesn't need complications now. Except for Aunt Lil's condition, things are going pretty well. He's saving some money, for one thing.

In Aunt Lil's room, Carl finds her sitting on the side of her bed, and before he can say anything, she asks him about the doctor's bill and the envelope she holds in her hand. She's thrown away the outside envelope, and the return envelope is missing, she says.

"You're holding the return envelope."

Aunt Lil looks down, then up. "Well, why won't this paper fit in it?"

"It will. See, it's fitting in there, and there's the doctor's address in the little window."

"No, I mean why won't the flap close? Here, try it."

"Okay. I'll do it. And then we need to talk about your driving."

"My driving?"

"That's right." Carl tries to close the flap, and sure enough, it won't close.

He takes the insert out, looks at it, realizes that if he tears off the return portion, that part will fit into the envelope, so he explains to Aunt Lil, hands the insert to her, and she tears off the return portion. As she puts it in the envelope, he thinks maybe he should somehow mention how much he likes Anna, but he's never talked to Aunt Lil about anything like that. And besides, he needs to talk about this driving issue.

"That whole business of driving off by yourself was a little dangerous, don't you think?"

"I have a driver's license. Why would they give me a driver's license if they don't think I can drive a car?" She is looking up at him from her seat on the side of the bed, a kind of angry glare in her eyes.

"You just don't have the reflexes and eyesight you used to have, Aunt Lil. You've been sick."

"Sick?"

"Your osteoporosis. All that pain. Falling in the bathtub. You know. You don't have the—"

"I can drive as good as you any day of the week. You know that, and listen, please tell me why there are so many charges on that bill, when all I had done is get my eyes checked."

"But that wasn't your car." The word *dementia* passes through Carl's mind.

"Well, it's an exact . . . what do you call it?"

"Replica."

"Yes. Now, why are there so many charges on that bill?"

Carl explains that all the writing is not for charges but for the times they billed Medicare and Blue Cross and it just looks like a lot of charges.

She complains about the bills that come in their own return envelope, so that you have to study the directions about how to rip off the edges on three sides in the right order and then get it folded up and back into itself and re-sealed somehow. And the writing is always light blue and very small. And she long ago gave up reading tiny directions on any pill or medicine bottle, she explains—even with a large magnifying glass.

"We need to put a check in there," says Carl, "for fif-teen dollars and four cents before we mail it back."

"Will you write it out?"

"Sure." He fills in the check and hands it to her to sign. This is probably a good time to simply tell her she needs to give up driving.

Her hand wobbles, and Carl looks away while she slowly signs her name.

As he takes the check, he sits down in the Kennedy rocker. "Aunt Lil, we need to talk about—"

"Wait a minute. I need to ask you something. Hillary Durham keeps writing me, and she's just a friend, and not even all that good a friend—you don't even know her—and she keeps sending me these little cards, and I used to write her every once in a while, but not as often as she writes me, and at the end of every one, she writes, 'I love you and the Lord loves you,' and I'm getting tired of it."

He can't tell if she's serious or trying to be funny.

She looks at him, straight-faced. "I just finished writing her a card," she says. "It took me all morning—I had to start over three times. I started to write, 'Love, Lil,' at the end of it, but I knew if I did that, then . . . that's not exactly true. I don't love her. Well, I love her well enough not to wish her any harm, but then again, I said to myself, Well, don't be so selfish, you old coot. Now, what do you think? Somehow I don't want to be getting gooey-gooey. I'm too old for that."

"Well, I don't know. I don't have any idea. I can think either way on that. There seem to be reasons to and reasons not to."

"Well, you're not much help. You need to be a little more decisive about things."

This is a first. "Okay. You wouldn't want this woman to start coming to see you all the time, would you?"

"Goodness, no."

"Well, that settles it. When in doubt, don't do it."

"Thank you." She starts to stand, doesn't make it, tries again, then again. She stands slowly. "Now, let's go eat. I can't wait to get some of that *fried chicken*. Yum, yum."

Why not tell her over lunch? That will be more comfortable. And she is ready to go.

ON THE WAY to the Piccadilly, Aunt Lil fishes out from her pocketbook the photograph of Mia Farrow she's been saving from *People* magazine. She says she wants a wig just like Mia Farrow's hair except it needs to be mostly silver with a brown tint. She says her old friend Emma Brown was upset she didn't get to sell Lil her first wig, so the plan is to go to Emma for a new one, after lunch.

At the Piccadilly, Aunt Lil gets fried chicken, string beans, and iced tea.

Carl gets slaw, meat loaf, mashed potatoes and gravy, broccoli and cheese, a slice of garlic toast, and a Diet Coke.

A cafeteria worker—his name tag says Delbert— carries Aunt Lil's tray ahead to their table.

Aunt Lil stops before they reach the table. "Have we eaten yet? Or are we about to eat?"

This is a little scary. "We're about to eat."

"I already got my food?"

"Yes ma'am. It's over there on the table."

"What did I get?"

"Fried chicken."

"Oh." She starts walking again. "I'm not surprised."

They settle in and Aunt Lil says the fellow who brought her food, Floyd, has been working at the Piccadilly for twenty years. He comes by again, Carl checks his name tag, and tells her it says Delbert.

"Well, his name is Floyd Delbert, then."

The next time he comes by, she stops him. "How long have you been working here, Floyd?"

He looks at his name tag, back at her. "About six months."

"I don't think so. You just don't remember. And you've lost about twenty pounds, haven't you?"

"No ma'am. I been weighing about the same for the last twenty years or so." He takes a step back and looks around.

"I think you just *think* you have."

"Well, that's okay." He picks up a tray on the next table, moves away.

After the meal, on his way to the cash register to pay with Aunt Lil's MasterCard, Carl realizes that he's forgotten to talk to her about the driving episode—the need to give up her license.

And on the way to A-1 Hair she wants to talk about Mr. Flowers, his plans to get some of the ladies on television. Should she buy a new dress? Will Carl be playing music with Mr. Flowers for good, now?

A-I HAIR DOES business from a large converted bungalow in a part of Summerlin Carl hasn't been to in years. But he knows all about the owner, Emma Brown, because every now and then Aunt Lil talks about Emma, her old business-school buddy, and her husband, J. M., who had a stroke some time back.

Just inside the front door is a foyer, with French door openings straight ahead, left, and right, but no actual doors. Inside, it smells like a damp basement and old magazines. The floor of the room on the left is covered with newspapers, magazines, and hair supplies, and dust. Just inside that doorway, fifteen or twenty phone books are stacked with a rotary phone on top. *Rotary* phone?

Carl leads Aunt Lil into the room straight ahead—a former hairdressing room, it looks like, but only one hairdressing chair is left, and that is full of hair supplies. And the smaller plastic chairs, around the walls, are mostly full of supplies. An elderly man is sitting in one of those. J. M.?

"Howdy," says Carl.

The man looks, but doesn't respond.

Mrs. Brown emerges from somewhere in back, holding a bottled Coke with a straw in it. "Hello . . . why, Lil! How in the world are you?" She hugs Lil over the walker.

"I'm not doing so good. I fell a while back and I've ended up out at Rosehaven for a while. This is my nephew, Carl."

"Yes, I've heard you talk about him. Of course. And Jo Ann Pitman told me about your fall. I'm so sorry to hear about that." She places the Coke with the straw on a stool beside J. M. He leans forward so he can drink without holding the bottle.

"I don't know what I'd do without Carl," says Aunt Lil.

"Oh, you're so lucky. What can we do for you today?"

"I want to buy me a wig like the one in this picture. The two I've had all these years are about worn out. Except my new one needs to be more or less gray, like I am—or used to be when I had my hair."

Emma holds the photo in her hands, turns it so the light is better. She doesn't seem upset about the other wigs. "I think we can help you out. You all sit down." She disappears through swinging doors into a back room.

Carl sits across the way from J. M., who nods his head. J. M. is not looking well.

Aunt Lil slowly eases herself down into the chair beside Carl. "J. M., how you been doing?" she says.

J. M. opens his mouth, but nothing comes.

Emma backs through the swinging door with a stack of four or five boxes. "Okay," she says to Aunt Lil, "I'll show you these one at a time, and you pick the one you like best." She lowers her stack of boxes onto a chair, opens the top box, reaches in, and pulls out a new wig— a tight little ball of hair. She holds it in her right hand, a couple of fingers on the inside, thumb on the outside, steps back to give herself room, stretches out her left arm for balance, like a dancer. Emma isn't young herself and is slightly humped. She slowly lifts the wig and then suddenly chops down—like a karate chop—and *whuff!* the wig is full and fluffy. She straightens up, looks at Carl with a light in her eyes. A few hairs float to the floor. She steps over to Aunt Lil and holds out the full wig in two hands.

"My Lord," says Aunt Lil.

J. M. sits up straight, grins. "She's a wig-popping mama."

Aunt Lil says, "That's exactly what I want. Let's put it on. That is something, the way you did that."

"Don't you want to check out these others?" Emma asks.

"Yeah," says Carl. "Let's see another one."

"No, this is the one I want."

"I just kind of want to see her open another one," says Carl. "That was something."

"Why?" says Emma. "Oh. Okay. Yes. Let's see another one. Been doing it forty-five years. Through thick and thin. You know—" she turns to Carl—"Lil had to go through looking after a sick husband too. It's not easy, is it, Lil?"

Carl wonders if J. M. can hear.

"No, it's not . . . This is the one I want. But yes. Yes,

let's do look at another one. Let me put this one on, though, and see how it looks."

Emma holds up a large hand mirror. Aunt Lil removes her old wig, pulls on the new one. "Oh, I like that. Don't you, Carl?"

"I sure do. Very becoming."

Emma straightens the wig, tucks a strand of Aunt Lil's hair.

Is there a song here somewhere? thinks Carl.

Emma opens another box, goes through her moves again, and this time Lil laughs, and so does Carl.

J. M. puts his hand on his head. "She's a wig-popping mama."

Carl writes a check to A-1 Hair for $41.17. Lil, sitting, signs it slowly. Emma tosses Lil's old wig into a trash can behind J. M.'s chair.

Outside, as he's about to open the passenger door for Aunt Lil, Carl stops, steps back—he'll try to make her laugh again—stretches out an arm, chops down with the other, and holds both hands out to Lil. She laughs a short laugh, and then *she* goes through the motions herself, and Carl says, "She's a wig-popping mama." Aunt Lil's head falls back; she looks into the sky as she laughs harder, then starts into the motion again and staggers in her walker as she keeps laughing. She looks at Carl and he sees that her eyes are wet.

• • •

Turning into the parking lot at Rosehaven, Carl faces a fact: he needs to stop by Anna's office. He doesn't feel good about it, sort of like he's visiting the doctor. After walking with Aunt Lil to her room, he continues on past the flower and fruit paintings in the hall, the supply closet, the bulletin board. He can't tell exactly how he feels or what he wants to happen. Anna's door is closed and there's a white envelope taped to it. His name is on it. Wow . . .

> Dear Carl,
>
> Things are not smooth in my life right now. I like you a lot and do not want to hurt our friendship, but the relationship that I am presently in and was in before our trip to the movie the other night is also very important to me. I will need to concentrate on that relationship for a while and I hope you understand. Please drop by and we can talk about this if you like.
>
> Sincerely,
>
> Anna

"Sincerely"? Well, that settles that. Drop by and talk about it? Right. He hadn't liked Anna's little girl all that much anyway, and besides, he hadn't even met the other one. Two children? That would be—would have been—impossible.

Part 3.

What About Carl?

Washington and Lee

L. RAY LOOKS ACROSS the front lawn from his wheelchair. Small, newly planted trees, staked with white ropes, stand here and there on the lawn. He and Faye, the physical therapist, have been discussing his condition. He was up to a seventy-five-degree bend more than a week ago. There's been no improvement since. L. Ray tells her it has seized somehow. She explains that with no improvement, therapy can't continue.

Mrs. Satterwhite—Beatrice—sits beside L. Ray. Beyond her are Lil and Clara. He decides to use their first names, now that they are the first disciples of his new movement.

He preached another sermon the night before, he and Carl played music, and now Beatrice has asked him how they are going to get their show on the road. The ladies seem interested, enthusiastic, as he'd hoped.

L. Ray leans forward, elbows on knees. "I think," he says, "the very first thing is to simply proclaim that churches and nursing homes should become one and the same. Some kind of public statement. Do a press conference."

"Think about the number of hours in a day," says Beatrice. "And think about the number of days in a week." She sees her way, through Flowers, to the doorstep of Walter Cronkite. She will explain what happened to the money he gave her and ask him to help patch things up with her son.

"Well, yes. But listen, if this plan works out, all sorts of problems, given our new ways of staying in touch with each other—cell phones, the Internet—can begin to get solved, in a kind of chain reaction."

Maybe she can get in touch with Walter Cronkite on the Internet. She sees a close-up of his face. She sees how tall he is, probably.

"And after old people," Mr. Flowers is saying, "old people who need help, we'll go with hungry children. They should be the first priority, but they can't vote or get mad about things the way old people will—I hope. We've got to get it structured just right, like the Wright brothers and that first airplane. They got all the angles just exactly right, and that thing lifted off."

Beatrice sees in her mind that picture of that old airplane lifting off on the beach up there at Kitty Hawk. Kitty Hawk. That's a funny name. Kitty Hawk. Kitty Hawk. Kitty Hawk.

"And the thing is," the preacher goes on, "it can get going the world over, on its own. A world movement can lead toward unity where there is none, peace where there is none, and harmony where there is none. And you know, already in many countries elderly people are respected lots more than among us proud-to-be-all-powerful Americans." He rolls his chair forward so he can see all three of them better. "And I want you to keep up your good singing," he says to Beatrice. "I'm going to get you on TV."

Beatrice envisions lights, cameras. She sings:

Softly and tenderly Jesus is calling . . .

"Now that's a good one," says Maudie, sitting down with them.

"Once it gets rolling, will we be able to travel places?" asks Lil.

"I don't see why not."

Lil sees herself in the Everglades, a place she's always wanted to visit. She will go to a nursing home down there, explain how easy it will be to make the place into a church for church people to visit on Sunday mornings. People like Mr. Grayson, with the lead poisoning, always swatting at butterflies, can have visitors every Sunday if something like that is started up.

"You're going to lose all the Christians," says little Maudie. "I can tell you that right now." She moves her shoulders forward then back so she can rock a bit.

There's one in every crowd, thinks L. Ray. "I'm not so sure. Some of them, maybe."

"You'll have a hard time with my niece, and me too."

Beatrice touches her gold mourning pin. "I love everybody. I think the whole world needs to change. I think there are too many companies. There's too much business. And on the television there's too much interference with life. It's like they turned loose a silly sideshow in every house in America. And besides all that, what you say you believe has nothing to do with how you live your life, and how you live your life is what Jesus watches. It's the same with our country. We say one thing, but look at what all these businesses do. And it's no telling what they do overseas where can't nobody see. They fire people exactly when they should help them—like a family helps. Companies are going to take over the world, like Hitler. You mark my words. Giant companies run out the little companies, and little companies are the backbone of a democracy. Giant companies are bullies because they're so big. If companies were run by people like Walter Cronkite, there wouldn't be as much evil in the world. Jesus wouldn't have run a company, because he didn't want to. Maybe John the Baptist would've. He could have sold some sewing machines, I'll bet."

"Nobody uses sewing machines anymore," says Maudie.

"Of course they do."

If I could get Beatrice off that Walter Cronkite kick, thinks L. Ray, she could be my right-hand man. "Whatever Jesus was, he was not a fundamentalist. Or whatever he is. I finally figured that out. Whoa. The fundamentalists were the ones always after him—the ones with all the laws written on their sleeves."

"Those were the Pharisees," says Maudie. "You got your math wrong."

"I want to generate an antifundamentalist righteous fervor that equals and then supersedes their own fervor, and I want this thing to be a movement of action, not words. If there's talk of telephone lines to God, we will simply stick our fingers in our ears and refuse to listen. Old people can be seen. My First Breakfasters will put action where their mouths are. I don't know, maybe I'm—"

"I think you'd better be careful," says Maudie. "You're starting some kind of government plan. You're getting way too big for your britches. Pride goeth before the fall."

"Maybe he'd better tiptoe through the tulips," says Beatrice.

L. Ray touches his hair. "No true visionary is careful. Look at Jesus. And read carefully what he says about us doing for each other."

"I think you ought to be careful," says Maudie.

"I'm too old for that. And I'm not interested in eternal life."

"That tells me you're interested in eternal damnation. The final days are near."

"I don't—"

"What are we going to fix to eat at the First Breakfast?" asks Lil.

Thank you, thinks L. Ray. "Oh, I don't know. I hadn't thought about it. Something good."

"What's a 'First Breakfast'?" asks Maudie.

"You know," says Clara. "Last Supper, First Breakfast."

"That's ridiculous."

"Why do you say that?"

"It just is."

"I know we probably won't have fried chicken for breakfast," says Lil, "but if you ever do, get the Piccadilly recipe. They have the best fried chicken."

"I'll remember that. We're going to have all kinds of good food."

"Oh, no," says Beatrice. She holds her newspaper up for Maudie to see. On the front page is Bill Clinton. "Look. It's him again."

"That nose—I think he's an alcoholic," says Maudie.

Well, thinks L. Ray, I held them for a while.

"He *was* the president, though," says Beatrice. "You've got to respect the office even if you don't respect the man in it. I think people made a devil out of him just because he wasn't the same kind of president as Washington and Lee and Lincoln."

"Lee?"

"Washington and Lee."

"I think I'll go in," says Maudie. She eases forward so her feet touch the floor and then stands slowly.

"That's a school," says Clara.

"What?" says Beatrice.

"Washington and Lee."

"Well, Lee was something."

"He was general of the Confederate army."

"I think he was president at some point."

"Grant was president, but not Lee," says Clara.

"He should have been."

"Not after being on the losing side."

"My uncle Benjamin lost a finger in that war," says Beatrice.

"Which one?" asks Clara.

"Index . . . they *said*."

"Which *war?*"

"Oh. Civil war."

"If it'd been my family, they wouldn't have known which one."

"Which what—war?"

"Finger."

Where's the song *here?* wonders L. Ray.

"I wonder why I've always heard 'Washington and Lee,'" says Beatrice.

"It's the name of a school."

"I wonder why they named it 'Washington and Lee' if Washington and Lee were on different sides."

"That was at different times," says Clara.

"What was different times?"

"Washington and Lee."

"Then why'd they name the school after them, do you suppose?"

"I don't know. I don't care to know."

"I don't think they'd name something 'Kennedy and Eisenhower' nowadays."

"No, they wouldn't. They just don't make them like they used to."

"And 'Washington and Lee' has a ring to it."

CARRIE AND LATRICIA are eating lunch on the picnic table behind the fence.

Latricia looks at the potato salad on her fork. "This stuff suck."

"That's why you ought to fix your own." Carrie thinks about offering half of her sandwich, decides against it.

"I don't have time, and this is free."

"Tell Mr. Rhodes about it."

"No way."

"I heard him talking to that deputy sheriff brought

back Mrs. Olive and them," says Carrie, "asking did he remember Mr. Flowers's IRS problems. I'll bet you soon as Mr. Flowers is about to stan' up on that leg, he be gone."

"The ladies'll miss him, I tell you that," says Latricia.

"They need Mr. Flowers down at Shady Rest." Carrie pictures the lunch room at Shady Rest, the patients' small rooms, a bed collapsed with poor Mrs. Terry asleep in it. "He'd start a ruckus down there."

"They need the sheriff down at Shady Rest. That's who they need down at Shady Rest."

Carrie drinks from her can of Diet Coke, swats at a fly. "Did you go in Mr. Andrews's room today?"

"No. But I'll tell you one thing: when he kick me, I kick him back."

"Somebody'll write you up too."

Latricia finishes her potato salad. "I don't care. Oh, listen. You know what Miss Avery told me?"

"What?"

"She told me the preacher man masturbated in front of her."

"Naw."

"She did. That's what she said."

"You don't believe it, do you?"

"Why would she come up with something like that?"

"She making that up. Something's not right about her." Carrie stretches her arms over her head. "I got to go in."

What About Carl?

ANNA DOESN'T KNOW what to do. Rhodes has asked her to keep an eye on L. Ray Flowers. And L. Ray's niece recently sent her a letter in support of institutionalizing L. Ray—something Anna has no control over. The niece, Gladys Jenkins, wrote about L. Ray's changing his name to William Searcy before heading to the Midwest as an evangelist many years earlier. And she enclosed a photocopy of an old newspaper clipping:

> Searcy is being sought by authorities after Silvia Parsons's husband filed a complaint yesterday. Parsons died after walking off a high stage while being "healed" by Mr. Searcy at a religious service in the Barry Winston Community

Center on Saturday night. Searcy was slowly walking forward across a high stage with his hands on Mrs. Parsons's head as she walked backward, when he stopped and stood still, the "miracle" finished. But she kept walking backward, off the stage, hit her head on the base of a flag stand, and died immediately. The drop from the stage was significant, about six feet, according to a videotape of the event obtained by WNCC. The station will play the tape on tonight's news broadcast at 6:00.

Because L. Ray brightens the lives of several of the ladies, Anna doesn't want to bring Mr. Rhodes up to date about L. Ray's past life. She doesn't want to tell Carl, either.

And what *about* Carl? He's come back around to talk since the note and didn't mention the note, but it had clearly hurt him. She should certainly talk about it, if he can't. She wishes she hadn't written it. And what about Danny? He wants to get married. He's a proven father, and a good one. He has a steady job and has recently been promoted. And he's commanding, in a way. She likes that. She imagines he'll be very good in bed, but she's not ready for that yet. Carl? In bed? He'd probably be looking at his hand the whole time. And she doesn't want to hurt Carl any more. In fact, with him, there are probably possibilities; he is so faithful to his aunt. How could he not make a good father? If *she* could get promoted —a couple of times—she wouldn't feel this strong need to get married, something she's afraid she's not ready for.

And should she tell anyone what Darla Avery has been saying? No. Clearly, it didn't happen.

Fat from Shame

"I DON'T THINK that's any of your business," little Maudie says to Beatrice. "I don't think anybody ought to be asking me about my bank account." She thrusts her head forward and gets her rocker going.

I wish they wouldn't fuss, thinks Lil.

"Well," says Beatrice, "we're all in this together, and somebody needs to be asking some questions. If we're going to travel with Mr. Flowers, then we'll need a little money."

Lil thinks about the Everglades. She will be able to see all kinds of exotic birds, birds with such bright colors.

"I'm not traveling with anybody," says Maudie, "especially him."

"Look how tall those trees are," says Beatrice.

"I don't know what you're talking about," says little Maudie.

"Oh, look, Lil, there's Carl," says Beatrice.

Lil is glad to see him but at the same time dreads a conversation about her driving. It's bound to come. Maybe if she went ahead and told him about that boy from Tad's first wife and how she feels betrayed—maybe he'd feel sorry for her a little bit. She doesn't want to beg, to beg about anything, but giving up driving would be the first mile of a highway that leads to a permanent spot at Rosehaven, and there is no good reason she knows of that she can't—in a few weeks, a month at the most—move back to her apartment and take up where she left off.

Little Maudie slips forward in her chair and slowly stands, reaching for her cane.

Carl is carrying a small paper bag of apples, which he hands to Lil. "I brought you a little something. Get you off them Tootsie Rolls. Hey there, Mrs. Lowe."

Maudie stops, turns, and speaks. "Afternoon, Carl. I'm going in. I'm tired of hearing about the preacher man."

The automatic front door closes behind Maudie, then opens, and a couple of aides emerge, headed home. Mrs. Talbert eyes their shoes, relieved that they are wearing white lace-ups. The other day, one came in wearing some kind of flip-flop things, and she'd rolled her chair all the way in to the admissions office and complained. And they said they'd do something about it too.

"Carl," says Beatrice, "have you heard Mr. Flowers's idea for a new song?"

"I don't think so."

One of the best things of all, thinks Lil, is that Carl is interested in playing music again.

"He's going to tell you all about it, I'm sure," says Beatrice. "It's the funniest thing. Here, sit down. He was sitting at our table last night. Maudie don't like him. He's started sitting at our table, and I'd cleaned my plate, and I says, 'My mama and daddy made us all clean our plates every meal we ever had, because they didn't want the first morsel to go to waste.' Because it's true, see—they did. All of us. And I'm *not* what you'd call thin. Never have been, really. So I looked at my plate and said what I always say. I said, 'I guess I'm just fat from shame.' And Mr. Flowers about died laughing, and, well, I want you to know he said he's going to get you to write a song called 'Fat from Shame.' I told him it could say, 'Fat from shame, my mama is to blame'!"

Lil thinks about her own upbringing. It was true in her house too. She notices that Clara has arrived.

Clara says, "That's Mr. Flowers's song he's going to get you to write, Carl. He's a something. I'm glad he's here, because this is one hell of a boring place. I had to stick myself with a needle to get something going around here yesterday."

"I wish you wouldn't talk like that, Clara," says Beatrice. "It's unbecoming."

Clara slowly lowers herself into the seat Maudie has just left. "I was in my bathroom and saw something shiny down on the floor and come to find out it was a straight pin. So I says to myself, I can't just leave that there. I've got to get it up. I held on to the back of the commode and bent down, but my fingers won't work worth a damn half the time, all knotted up like they are. So I tried first one thing and then the other. I tried dropping a blouse down on it and then picking up the blouse, but that didn't work."

I would have got down on my knees and back up again, thinks Lil.

"So then I realized that if I took that commode extender off the commode seat and sat down on the commode, I could bend over and reach it while I was sitting down, and not hurt my legs so much. So I did that. But I still couldn't reach it, because I'd pushed it away. But then I was so low to the floor, sitting down, I couldn't get up, and I knew I was going to have to pull that damn cord.

"Then I decided that I wouldn't pull the cord until I got the pin up. Which was a mistake. Had I been thinking, I'd pulled the cord first. So anyway, I started working on it again. Then I got my idea: Step on the goddamned thing. Get it up that way. I got them thick-ass calluses on the bottom of my feet."

"Clara!" says Beatrice. "My stars."

"So that's what I did—worked my foot a little bit, and

here comes the pin, stuck in that big callus, but not deep enough to hurt, see. What the hell am I going to do now? I says. I can't reach my foot. That's when I pulled the cord. And nobody came. Which is why I should have done that first. I pulled it again, and finally somebody comes and gets the pin out of my foot, and they want to know how in the world it got in there. I didn't even bother to tell the whole story."

"My goodness," says Beatrice, "you were in a real predicament. Why didn't you just pull the cord for them to come get the pin up off the floor?"

"Well . . . because I wanted to do it myself. That's what's wrong with so many old people. Or just people. There's more laziness around here than birds."

"You know," says Beatrice, "I don't honestly see how you can see so good."

"My good eye is one hell of a good eye. That's how."

"Can I ask you a question?"

No, not that, thinks Lil.

"Sure," says Clara.

". . . Never mind."

"What is it?"

"Nothing. I forgot."

"So," says Clara, "when are you going to take us shopping again, Lil?"

"Oh, I don't know." She looks at Carl to see if he has heard. She doesn't want any driving talk. "I would like to go shopping again, though." She does not want any driving talk. "Maybe we can find that flag."

"I might get me another lawn chair," says Clara. "I can fold them up and put them in the closet until all my nieces and nephews come at the same time. Except if one did happen to show up, I'd be so surprised I think I'd drop dead."

Inside, Lil sits in her La-Z-Boy and Carl sits in the Kennedy rocker. He glances at the steady wobble of her hand.

"Now, how much money did you say I have?" Lil asks.

"Around ninety-five thousand dollars total, when you cash in those war bonds."

She stares at him as if she were working on a puzzle. "And how much rent do I have to pay?"

"For here?"

"No. My apartment."

"I don't know. It's drawn automatically from your checking account. I can't remember. Around eight hundred a month, I think."

"It's more than that here, isn't it?"

"Considerably. Yes." He thinks about getting some kind of power of attorney, but since she can still sign her name and has her wits about her, more or less, he figures there's no need to rush it. All that could be embarrassing to her. It was to his mother.

"Ninety-five *thousand?*" she says, frowning at him as though she can hardly believe it. Her wig is a little bit off to one side.

"You need to straighten your wig. Turn it this way just a little. No, the other way. Good. Yes ma'am. Five CDs with ten to fifteen thousand in each one, and the bank says those bonds are worth about thirty thousand, and then about five thousand in your checking account."

"That's not so bad, is it?"

"No ma'am, it's not."

"Thank goodness for Tad's pension."

"Yeah, well, the government does that. I think the post office is pretty good to its people. How long did he work there?"

She looks at him with a kind of frown, and says, "Did you bring my Tootsie Rolls?"

"No, you've got Tootsie Rolls over there. I brought a few apples."

"Will you bring me my file box from the apartment?"

"I forgot about it. I sure will."

"I need to go through it. Don't you want an apple?"

"Sure, I'll take one."

"How about that 'Fat from' . . . what is it?"

"Shame."

"Are you going to write another song?"

"I guess, as long as L. Ray keeps collecting ideas."

"Collecting items?"

"Collecting ideas."

"IDs?"

"*Ideas.*"

"Oh . . . collecting *ideas*. For what?"

"For songs."

"I guess he is. Would you put that box of Kleenex over here? Wonder who invented Kleenex."

"I don't know."

"What did I pay for this wig?"

"About forty dollars. Why?" Carl wonders why she's so talkative. Have they given her some kind of medication?

"I want to give Reverend Flowers some money for his new religion."

"Has he asked you for money?"

"Oh, no. No. But Clara thinks he's on to something with his new religion, or whatever it is. And I do too. Once he gets it started, we might get a chance to travel a little bit, and I want to help him out. Clara thinks he hung the moon and we've been talking about ways to help him out. That little Maudie don't like him. You've met him, haven't you?"

"Yes, of course. We were just talking to him. Just now out on the porch. We've been with him out there several times, and he's teaching me to play bass guitar—or taught me. You know, all the songwriting?" Carl notices one of her eyelids is drooping. It hasn't been like that, has it? A tiny stroke?

"That's right. That's right. Yes. I remember. Well, he's so 'determed,' like Uncle Sorrell used to say, and sincere, and well grounded. What do you think about him?"

"I think it's going to take a little more to start a world religion, or movement, or whatever it is, than just a few people. I think he may be a little bit off his rocker, actually. On that, anyway."

"Well, I admire somebody who goes after what they want. Hand me my checkbook."

"How much do you want to give him?"

"I don't know. What do you think?"

"I don't know."

"Well, you ought to have some idea."

"I'm just not sure about giving him money."

"I thought you liked him."

"I do."

"Well, give me a number."

"Ten dollars?"

"Oh. Okay. Write it out and I'll sign it."

Carl writes the check. She signs it very slowly, then asks Carl to pass it on to Mr. Flowers. "And listen," she says, "I been aiming to ask you to bring me that metal file box in the bedroom closet and let me look through it. I've about forgot what all I got in there."

"Okay. We just decided that."

"And I want to look at my will. Did I tell you my will leaves everything I got to you?"

"No ma'am, you didn't. I appreciate it." Carl thinks about what he might do with sixty or seventy thousand dollars. New truck. But she might keep living and run out of money. At the present rate she'll run out of money in just a few years. And she can easily live that long. If he completely neglects her, she won't live as long as if he keeps looking after her. Now where in the world did that come from? he thinks.

"You've been good to me," she says. "I always wanted a child of my own, but it never worked out that way. Now I'd like to give some money to Mr. Flowers."

"We just did that."

"Oh. Okay. How much?"

"Ten dollars."

"Is that all?"

"Well, we've already written the check. See?"

"Oh. Margie Lee's husband forgot just about everything he ever knew and ended up driving to Traveler's Rest that day, and she had to go get him. You remember that?"

"I sure do. And look, that reminds me: we need to talk about this whole business of driving."

"It was such an awful thing. Nobody knew where he was."

Carl notices that she's looking at the door, not at him. She turns her head, looks at him, and frowns. "Carl, you know good and well I can drive as good as you can. The government gave me my license and hasn't seen reason to take it. I want you to let me drive out in the country some, where there's not so much traffic. Out to the lake, maybe. Can we do that one day? You'll be with me. I don't like driving in a parking lot, for goodness' sakes."

"Well . . . I don't know."

"It's the saddest thing, and I'm so glad Mr. Flowers is looking into all that."

"Into what?"

"Getting some help for old people. People, visitors, come in here and won't even look at you. I thank the Lord for you every day."

"Well, I'm glad to do what I can."

"And I want you to get some kind of safe in here—a little safe with a combination, because I'm missing some Tootsie Rolls and a pen. So see how much a little safe costs. Now, I think I need a little nap."

"Well, we don't . . . you don't have to give up on your apartment right yet. You know, we said we'd see what the doctor says. You get you a nap, and I'll see you soon." There is some way he can't name in which he doesn't want her to give up. But in another way he does.

As he leaves, Carl finds Mrs. Talbert in her wheelchair, sitting just outside the front door, as usual. He thinks of concrete lions set onto the stoops of courthouses. Where is the pale lady, the one usually by the wall?

Mr. Rhodes, just out of his big black car, parked beneath the drive-under, is coming toward him. "Mr. Turnage, can we sit here on the porch just a minute, if you have time?"

"Sure."

Mr. Rhodes leads Carl to two rockers.

"Now, Mr. Turnage, in my business, controversy hurts —big-time. I don't mind our assisting Mr. Flowers, but Mr. Flowers now knows where I stand and so that's that. You may or may not be aware of his past troubles."

"No, I'm not. I—"

"Mr. Rhodes?" Mrs. Lowe's niece, Emily, has walked up. "My aunt would like to get—oh, I'm sorry. Am I interrupting?"

"No problem," says Mr. Rhodes, standing. "What can I do for you?"

Carl stands and steps away. He doesn't like Emily. She's too gushy. She reminds him of his high school chemistry teacher, who dressed the same way: long, loose purple, orange, or blue skirts and blouses and substantial clay jewelry. Chemistry is where he used to go to sleep all the time, because she didn't care. What was her name? He'd wake up, and drool had run down his desk and left a big wet circle on his shirt. That was some good sleeping.

Traci, an aide, stops on the way to the parking lot, speaks to Emily. Mr. Rhodes starts toward his car.

Emily is saying something to Traci about the brain's

being like an onion. Carl decides he'll do what Flowers does—listen in for a song idea. He sits down in a rocker, close enough to hear.

"It starts to wither more or less from the outside," says Emily, "and so the inside is preserved and you can remember from way back, but because the outside is damaged from lack of oxygen and all, you can't remember some of what happened the day before, or in the last hour or few seconds. She's repeating right bad."

Mrs. Talbert rolls her wheelchair over and asks the nephew, "What did she say?" This man has the nicest pair of lace-up shoes, and he's such a loyal visitor.

"Wither. Something starts to wither in your brain." This is the first time Carl remembers seeing her away from the door.

"Something's withering about me too. My legs burn all the time, down toward my ankles."

I certainly can't get anything from this, thinks Carl—for a song. And I don't know if I even should.

"You ever tried Cetaphil?" Emily asks Mrs. Talbert.

"No. They don't make nothing for the skin that's any good anymore. Not since Palmer's. I don't think they can do any more for my legs. And that osteoporosis is not something that gets better. I got it all over the place." She holds up her hands. "I got it in my fingers."

Carl wants to get back to work. He looks at his watch, stands, then sees Mrs. Satterwhite—Beatrice—pushing her three-wheeler out through the door. He sits back down.

"What's 'dot-com'?" Beatrice asks Emily. "They keep saying it on television."

"It's like an address—it's part of an address. Did you know you can send a letter through a computer now? That's all it is, part of an address. It's like, well, the E-mail comes through a telephone line, and a telephone line these days can transfer writing and pictures."

"I don't see how they get it in there," says Beatrice.

"It's a quandary," says Mrs. Talbert.

"It's a quandary," thinks Carl. That's a line—a title. He tries it. Then something about the laundry? No. No good.

"Not really," says Emily. "The lines carry electrical impulses. A line can be one hundredth the width of a single hair, and it's not paper that it carries, it's electrical impulses, which get translated into letters—words and letters."

Carl stands.

"It has to do with electric current and the speed of light," says Emily. "All this is moving so fast it—"

"Have you ever thought about this?" says Beatrice. "There's a buildup, buildup, buildup, of electricity. It just keeps building up and building up and building up."

Carl sits again.

Beatrice turns and looks at Carl. "And it's all going to just explode, *ka-wham,* and that's going to be the end of the world. Late at night when I cut off the TV, I can see a little flicker in there—after the TV has already been cut off. There it is—a little flicker of electricity in there—but the thing is already *cut off*. That stuff is building up, building up, building up. All over the place."

"Cars are so complicated now, nobody knows how to fix them," says Traci.

Out rolls L. Ray. He nods to Carl, "Hey, buddy."

"Howdy." Carl checks his watch again. He'll leave the song-title-getting to L. Ray. He needs to go to work. He stands.

"My car broke down yesterday," says Emily, "and within five minutes a wrecker drove by with the nicest black man driving, and he took me and my car straight to my mechanic and I don't think he even charged me the full fee. God was there for me in my time of need. He hasn't failed me yet."

L. Ray says, "You know, Emily, I used to think that very same thing. I used to preach that very same thing, until I read about a child dying of leukemia and I got to thinking and I . . ."

Carl sits back down, picks up a newspaper, and pretends to read.

"I tried to summon up God, and I realized all of a sudden that every time God is helping *me*, some little child or baby is dying somewhere on earth, a bunch of them, as a matter of simple fact—guiltless children, frightened children, children dying with that fright still in their eyes. I mean death hits, *bam,* while a little baby is still scared, *bam,* Mr. Death, that is, Mr. Prince of Darkness, Mr. Void, Mr. Finality, Mr. That's All She Wrote. He—now forget about the baby, think right *here*—he's practically always corridored behind these doors at Rosehaven, or worse still, down at Shady Rest, lurking, waiting for a chance to barajarum in through a door and grab up somebody. Swoosh in lightly. Whoosh out bearing that heavy soul bound for the fiery internal void of boundless hollow black space, and sometimes that slack-jawed sore-gummed seventy-nine-pound very old lady is awake before she dies, with her eyes saying, Save me save me save me—her eyes darting from you to the somebody standing back there behind you. Then back to you. And sometimes they unconscious, sometimes they be thrashing around, done thrashed outen they clothes like a woman hit on a motorcycle leaving her shoes, and you wonder how she can be hit hard enough to leave her shoes at the wreck while she be way over yonder in the woods. And then that final long fifty seconds or two minutes or one or two hours that little lady be laying there on the sheets, laying on her final sheet change, her final sheet with 'Hall 3' marked on a sheet corner in black Magic Marker, and doing her dead-level best to get one last, last . . . one last breath. Then finally a breath do not come and the last one is the very, the ultimate, the last squeaked in, the puff, the sputter, the oh-my-this-is-it last one forever, sister. No, no, no. All that is normal death. I'm talking about that same Mr. Death, Mr. Void, Mr. Prince of Darkness, taking a little helpless baby who's never thought nothing wrong, nothing bad, nothing sinful, never done nothing but breathed, and so I, personally . . ."

Carl is embarrassed by the emotion of the message-giving. He looks from his newspaper without moving his head. L. Ray is staring up at Emily, fingers of one hand resting against his chest, talking with his other hand, and kind of twitching around in his seat.

". . . I just can't make all that work together—the stuff you just said, the stuff about God looking after some-body *personally* with all the bad stuff that's going on everywhere. I think it's sad that fundamentalists—you pick the religion—have got the one true track to God, the one and only true track of all the ways of worship on earth. No fundamentalist is tolerant." He keeps looking at Emily. "That I know of."

"Well, I don't know about that, Mr. Flowers. I'm not sure you have much ground to stand on." Emily turns to Mrs. Olive's nephew, now looking up at her. "I believe in a personal God. Don't you?" she says to him. She feels desperate, angry, and knows her face is flushed. She needs some support, some backup from this *normal* man.

Carl answers, "Well, I guess. I believe in the Bible and God and Jesus and all the things I grew up with, and I do like the old hymns." He can't give her exactly what she wants, he knows. He isn't even sure what he believes in. He can't remember being asked.

L. Ray asks Emily, "Do you go to Listre Baptist?"

"Yes, I do." She glares at him.

"You all have missionary families going to England and Alaska and South Africa, don't you?"

"We have partnerships with Baptists in other countries and we try to—"

"It seems like church members often have a desperate need to be *un*aware of the local needs of the local wrecks of local women stacked along the local grim halls of local nursing homes, places in conditions far sadder than merry Rosehaven—places like Shady Rest. I read about lay missionaries off to Alaska, where paid church workers are already on station."

"I am a—"

"Off to Alaska," Flowers sings. "You're off to Alaska to see some other Baptists. It blows my mind. WWJD? Why, yes, he'd go to Alaska."

He is ranting again. Carl looks at his watch.

"I'm a caretaker, Mr. Flowers," says Emily. "My aunt is up here. And in my church we have people assigned to elderly people, to help them, and—"

"You know what, Mrs. . . . . I'm sorry."

"McPherson. Emily McPherson."

"Mrs. McPherson, I am very sorry. I apologize. I need to stop lecturing. I am forever turning good people against me. I know you're doing what you can for the Lord, and the fact that you're even doing anything, whether we agree about it or not, is a kind of miracle in itself. I'm sorry."

Emily stands, staring at L. Ray. She opens her mouth, closes it, looks at Carl, looks back to L. Ray, and says, "You sick redneck. Riding your high horse . . . You Unitarian."

"Them are a poor excuse for shoes, if you ask me," says Mrs. Talbert to Emily.

"Excuse me?"

But Mrs. Talbert is on the way back to her spot by the door.

Emily turns—her clay jewelry jangles—and heads for the parking lot.

Carl decides he'll try something with L. Ray. He'll tell him what he's thinking. "I don't think the whole subject of God is something people are going to change their minds about. There's just something about it that—"

"Well, they should."

"Will you change your mind?"

"Most certainly. I have. I didn't know you'd thought about all this."

"I hadn't till just now," says Carl, "much. It's too deep for me."

"What do you suggest?"

Carl remembers a joke. "Did you hear about the grand-son who went to see his grandma and she didn't know who he was, and he said, 'Grandma, I'm David, your daughter's son.' She says, 'Who?' He says, 'You know your daughter, Betty, don't you?' And she says, 'Yes.' And he kind of points at himself and says, 'Well, I'm David, her son, and that makes me your grandson.' She looks at him a minute and says, 'That's too deep for me.'"

"Ah," says L. Ray. "And that's exactly one of my points."

I don't want to hear one of your points, thinks Carl.

"If it's not obvious," says L. Ray, "if it has something to do with something that's not obvious, why talk about that, when there are all these grim halls and all this work and a surefire way to get it all started—when there's all that work to talk about?"

"Well, that's a good question. Speaking of that, I've got to get to work. I was trying to pick up a song idea, but nothing hit me."

"I got one for you: 'Fat from Shame.' I was—"

"I heard about it already."

Lunch at the Piccadilly

ON THE WAY TO Rosehaven to pick up his aunt
Lil and Mrs. Cochran to take them to the Piccadilly for
lunch, Carl gets the idea that he ought to look through
Aunt Lil's file box. It's beside him on the front seat of the
Taurus. He stops at Burley's Exxon and sits for a minute
with the air conditioner on and finishes listening to a song
on the radio. Then he presses the button lock, and the
box opens. Inside are manila folders labeled BANK, IN-
SURANCE, PICTURES, and TAXES, and one that says PRI-
VATE. He figures he'll just hand that one to her, but then
he figures he can glance in. He pulls it out.

There are five or six letters in envelopes, it looks like,
and something has been torn up and dropped in there. He
grabs a piece of it: thick paper, nice, old paper, once torn

up and balled up, then flattened out. Or balled up first, then torn up.

He gets out all the pieces, puts the file box in the floorboard, and starts fitting the pieces together on the seat, like a puzzle. He sees that it's a certificate of marriage, Aunt Lil and Uncle Tad's. What is this about? He puts the pieces back in their folder and closes the box. No need to bother anything. He's not even sure why he's looking in there.

CARL PULLS UP in the Rosehaven parking lot. A rescue squad van is parked under the roof at the porch entrance. As he gets out of his car, the van drives off.

Anna is in the lobby talking to a middle-aged couple, and when she sees him, she nods, and he knows it's not his aunt Lil the rescue squad has come for.

When he gets to her room, Aunt Lil is standing by her window, looking out. A hammer lies on her bed. She turns and looks at Carl. She is dressed for the Piccadilly, except her wig is not on and her sparse hair stands out every which way.

"Hey, there," he says, and puts the file box down by her La-Z-Boy.

She slowly sits down on the bed. "Time is the strangest thing. It pulls up into a little bunch and just sits there, not even spread out anymore, and all the people you've ever known—mothers you remember from way, way back, and their babies, babies you remember, babies becoming mothers and then *grand*mothers—all of it gets wrapped up in a little bunch that seems about a year or two old, and it's all right there behind you. It just stops being all stretched out for some reason. Beatrice got carried to the hospital today. She had a stroke, and it made me start thinking back over things, start trying to think back over things."

Carl pictures Beatrice sitting on that seat in her three-wheeled walker, touching her gold pin. "I'm sorry to hear that. You know, one thing I've wondered—where do you think she got all that about Walter Cronkite and her son?"

"I guess it happened."

"Really?"

"Why not?"

"I don't know, I just . . . Do you still want to go to the Piccadilly?"

"Yep." She stands slowly and, in front of the mirror, holds her wig above her head, pulls it on, straightens it, then reaches for her walker. "But let me tell you what I did. I had that picture of me and the business-school girls to put up, so they brought me a hammer and I tried to nail that little hook thing *into the back of the picture frame* . . . I was trying to get it to work, and I kept saying to myself, Something's not right."

"I see. Yeah, that wouldn't work all that well."

"So I finally just went out and found Anna, and she sent Roman down here to hang it up. Doesn't it look nice?"

"It does."

"Now, what did you just ask me?"

"Do you still want to go to the Piccadilly?"

"Yes. Clara's going. And I invited Mr. Flowers to go along."

"To the Piccadilly?"

"Yes, he's had some bad luck. Somebody says they're running him out, and I can't imagine why. I tried to ask Anna, but she wouldn't talk about it."

In a few minutes, Carl opens the door to L. Ray's room. Straight ahead are double windows with Venetian blinds closed against a bright sun. L. Ray sits in his wheelchair with his back to the windows. He wears a navy blue T-shirt. The room has been completely rearranged; earlier, the bed was by the windows. "Hey there," says Carl. "I'm sorry about your bad luck. I'm getting ready to take Aunt Lil up to the Piccadilly and she asked me to come get you, but don't feel obliged if you're not in a notion to go."

L. Ray smiles. "With you and Mrs. Olive and Mrs. Cochran to the Piccadilly? Of course. I'll meet you in the lobby. I guess you heard about Beatrice—Mrs. Satter-white?"

"I heard."

"It's sad. She's a main supporter. Rhodes is saying I've exposed myself to somebody up here, and that's all the information I can get. I don't understand. And please don't tell the ladies."

"Damn." What in the world? Would he do that?

"But they can't keep me from visiting, from coming back, without some kind of restraining order. From keeping things rolling. And we'll keep playing music for the ladies. It's a free country—unless you're old and in the way."

"Well . . ." Carl can't think of a thing to say. "Do you know that song, 'Old and In the Way'?"

"Great song. Jerry Garcia."

"I think David Grisman wrote that one."

"Maybe so. That would be a good one to learn, anyway." L. Ray reaches for a shirt. "We'll see you in the lobby in a few minutes."

As Carl leaves, he meets Anna and a . . . the policeman.

"Carl, this is Danny."

"Howdy," says Carl.

They shake hands.

"My pleasure. Are you a relative of Mr. Flowers's?"

"No. Just a friend."

"Danny's here on business," says Anna. "He's delivering a, uh . . . an eviction notice to Mr. Flowers. Mr. Rhodes gave him a week."

"Where'd they get this exposing himself stuff?" He glances at the policeman, then back at Anna.

"I'm not supposed to say," says Anna. "Nor is Danny."

• • •

RIDING TO THE PICCADILLY, they pass a badly crushed automobile that has not been towed from the accident site. Carl thinks about the conversation he needs to have with Aunt Lil, once and for all. Not now, though. She's in back with Mrs. Cochran. L. Ray is up front with him.

"Mr. Flowers," says Aunt Lil, "did they ask you to leave?"

"Oh, no. My time is up. My leg is about well. I'll be heading home in the next week or so. But I'll be coming back to visit you ladies. We can't desert our movement."

"I'll say not," says Mrs. Cochran.

Along about the Triple A Rent-All, Aunt Lil says, "When do you think it might be time to travel some?"

"It shouldn't be too long. Once we get the news out there, get some financing, we'll be on the road."

"Lil," says Mrs. Cochran, "you can drive the van."

"That'd be fun," says Lil.

She'd do it, thinks Carl.

"You'd run all the red lights between here and Florida," says Mrs. Cochran, "and they'd put us in prison—which reminds me, I want you all to listen to this: My husband, Martin, heard from a prison guard one time this story about a prisoner who somehow had the whole bottom half of his face torn off, from just below his eyes. I think it was some kind of farm machine he got caught in, or something blew up in his face or something, you know, where they work on the farm—the prisoners. They fixed him up in the prison hospital as good as they could."

I wonder what she did in her former life, thinks Carl.

"I don't know if the accident happened before or after he got in prison," continues Mrs. Cochran. "Well, time passed, and he said he sure missed his nose and he sure would like to have a new one. So what they did was they rolled up a roll of fat on his stomach or somewhere and tied it off so that it wouldn't die and rot off. A roll of fat about the size of a big nose, and somehow . . . somehow they could move it on up toward his face. Over a period of time. You know, just somehow move it along a fraction of an inch every few days, Martin said. Don't ask me how. Finally, after a long time he had a nose."

"Oh, mercy me," says Aunt Lil. "They just moved it along?"

"I guess."

"How in the world did they get it up to right above his mouth?"

"You mean, where his mouth used to be."

"Yes."

"Well, I don't know. Hadn't thought about that. Maybe they took it on around behind his head, up his neck, over the top of his head, and then down between his eyes."

"Lord have mercy," says Aunt Lil. "Wouldn't it have gotten hair growing out of it while it was coming up over his head?"

"I don't know. I never heard. But . . . you know, what about this: do you reckon they used his navel as a nostril?"

"Oh, my goodness, Clara."

Carl laughs. He's never . . .

L. Ray unsnaps his seat belt and turns around in his seat, laughing, and after a minute he's telling a story he heard, and the way he tells the story, his excitement, the way he communicates with those two ladies—after being asked to leave Rosehaven—somehow begins to convince Carl that maybe there *is* something to L. Ray's preaching, something to his movement. Maybe he's more sincere than Carl has imagined. But what about this exposing himself story? Where would that—

"And that little boy," says L. Ray, "had skin grafted onto his hand from the burn, and this is back when they had to attach things to get skin grafted, and they attached this boy's hand to his lower stomach, and five or six years later his hand starts growing pubic hair." L. Ray laughs. Aunt Lil and Mrs. Cochran laugh. Carl can't help himself; he laughs again, wondering what's so funny. What a strange story. He senses that Aunt Lil and Mrs. Cochran would follow L. Ray anywhere.

They unload at the mall. Carl parks the car.

In the Piccadilly, Aunt Lil gets fried chicken, string beans, and rice. Mrs. Cochran gets fish and vegetables. L. Ray gets two beet salads, black beans and rice. Carl gets fried chicken, mashed potatoes, cole slaw, and a cottage cheese salad. Everybody gets sweet iced tea, and Carl gets Diet Coke.

One of the staff helps with trays, and they all end up sitting in the smoking section, close to the place Lil and Carl usually sit, against the wall.

"You say the blessing," Lil says to L. Ray. "You're the preacher."

"Well, let's see. I'd like to use a little portion of a new sermon I've been working on, if that's okay." He closes his eyes. *"O God in us all, may we embrace the rooms of refuge food. Real food, cheap food, food served by people with wet rags under their arms. I eat; I cheat. I forge; I gorge. I taste; I waste. Waffle House, Huddle House, Puddle House, Muddle House."*

Carl opens his eyes and watches him.

L. Ray's head leans back just a little, eyes closed, trancelike. *"Oh, the dying and bygone potential union of blacks and rednecks, once a thread of certain words like* draw *for* drawer, *as in 'Get the pie from the draw over there,' and* hongry *for* hungry, *as in 'I'm hongry,' once a thread, food thread or not, always frazzled, a thread of religion and family habits and knowledge of geography, now frayed beyond repair and only redeemable in the fading mist of this new century, redeemable through cabbage, collards, turnip salet, fried fatback, the slunken foods now reserved for movies and poverty . . ."*

Carl looks around to see if people are looking; no one is.

"*. . . and selected sanitation-grade B cafeterias and some small farms and old evaporated dreams of slack-jawed beggars. Help us, O God in us all, help us reinvent, remember, the proper cooking of foods of the home, foods that feed our attitudes and make bonds where none will otherwise be, foods from the childhoods of old people that will bring to their hearts—through their mouths—precious memories. We church people must bring these foods to old people as we transform nursing homes into churches. Make us ministers of memory.*"

Carl shifts in his chair, closes his eyes again. When will this end?

"*We need real corn bread. We need a homemade tortilla. May we, with powerful spirits, diminish the force of fast food. Give victory to thy forces as we come to fight with the forces that will put man-made genes into the food that has until the last decade been sanctified by the breath of the Holy Spirit of the Holy Universe of Soft Green Fields. Amen, and amen.*"

"Amen," says Aunt Lil.

"That was a long blessing," says Mrs. Cochran. "I like that part about corn bread. I like anything about corn bread. They've completely ruint corn bread. I had nineteen recipes for corn bread that came out of the *Farmers' Almanac*. I need some hot sauce. Texas Pete. Oh, there it is." She turns to L. Ray. "I wish you weren't leaving us."

"I do too," says Aunt Lil. "I'm getting used to having you around."

Carl starts to cut his chicken with a knife and fork, looks at Aunt Lil to see if she's going to pick her chicken up.

"The best way to eat chicken," says L. Ray, "if you're not going to pick it up, is with two forks."

"Pick it up," says Mrs. Cochran. "We're among friends."

"Amen," says Aunt Lil.

The File Box

AUNT LIL STANDS IN HER ROOM, pointing. "Put it on that footstool, and let me look through it for a minute or two. There might be something in here that I . . ."

Carl places the file box on the footstool, open. She sits slowly, begins pulling out the files, peeking in each one, then putting it in her lap. He wonders if she'll mention the marriage certificate.

"I want you to go through this one"—she hands him a folder—"and throw away anything over three years old." She sorts. "Now this one, this one should have something in it that . . ." She opens it and collects a few pieces of the marriage certificate, then puts them back and hands the folder to Carl. "I want you to get out those torn-up pieces in there, please, and then I want you to put them back together on a piece of cardboard that's the same size and flatten them in a book and glue them back together as much as you can. I've thought about that and thought about it and thought about it. That's all. I've decided what I want to do about it."

"I'll do it."

Both her hands are suddenly over her face.

"What's the matter?" He notices how crooked her little fingers are. He's never noticed that. Or maybe that's new. Is she laughing, or crying?

"Nothing," she says.

"Yes, there is too. What's the matter?"

She's having a hard time getting her breath. She drops her hands and looks straight into Carl's face. Her red eyes hold water. "He did a terrible thing."

"Who?"

"Tad."

"What? What did he do?"

She looks out the window. "Can we go out and smoke us one?"

"Sure."

On the porch, they get settled. Nobody else is around. She starts talking, working a tissue in one hand, holding her cigarette in the other. "He had a son."

"Uncle Tad?"

"Yes. It wasn't his. It was his wife's—the wife before me. Her name was Alice. Her husband drowned when she was six months pregnant. She'd already had the baby when she met Tad, but Tad wouldn't marry her if she kept the baby, of all things—can you imagine?—so she had him adopted down to Florida, and the boy, after he grew up, came to our house looking for Tad. He was eighteen years old. That's when I heard the whole story. And the boy had been through a horrible time working in orange groves all his life. What kind of mother would do something like that? And what kind of man would ask her to?" She balls up the tissue in her fist, sticks out her chin.

He's never seen her angry—or hardly ever. Nor his aunt Sarah. Well, not even his mother, except when he was little. Was that . . . was that why it was easy to take care of them? "Where was she—the mother—all this time?"

"Well, she died of cancer after she and Tad had been married about five years. That's the only part I knew about beforehand, and the boy hadn't known about that till he was grown. His real daddy's sisters told him all about it, once he tracked them down, and then he comes looking for Tad, but Tad wouldn't even talk to him. See, Tad married me very soon after Alice died, and I never knew a thing about a boy, a baby—any of that."

"Why didn't I know about all this? Mother knew about it, didn't she?"

"Well, yes, but she and Sarah knew I wanted to forget it all."

"I wouldn't have thought anything bad about it— about you."

"I know. I know. See, I had time enough left to have a

child or two when we got married, and I'd always dreamed of that. I always wanted children, always thought about it, hoped for it."

Carl stands. Why hadn't they let him in on something like this? Why hide it? He half sits on the porch rail.

"And then," she says, "when I met Tad and he asked me to marry him, I figured I still had a chance to have a baby, but we never talked about it, because nobody ever talked about things in my family or his, I guess, and we got married, and he said he didn't want any children, and when I got up the nerve to say I'd always wanted a baby, he said, well, I'd have to get divorced and marry some-body else, he reckoned, and then he tried to make a big joke out of it and talk about all the work it would be—more trouble than it was ever worth, he said—and how the whole business was unnecessary and troublesome. And that was the end of that."

"Why did you stay with him?"

"Why did I stay with him?" She stares at Carl.

"Right. Why did you stay with him?"

"I don't know." She looks down into her lap and then out across the lawn. "I couldn't leave him. I just couldn't. Nobody did that. In my family. You haven't been mar-ried, yet. And . . . and I couldn't argue with him. That just is not something I was made up to do. Look, there's that little squirrel. I was out here the other day and—"

"Aunt Lil, you were talking about not being able to ar-gue with Uncle Tad."

"Oh, yes. I wasn't able to stand up for myself somehow. None of us were, in a way, and I don't want that drifting on down to you."

"I think I stand up for myself." How can I stand up to people who are hiding things? he thinks.

"Then after we'd been married a long time, the young man knocked on our door, and by this time we'd had a pretty good marriage. Well . . . no, it wasn't a pretty good marriage. It was a tolerable marriage. At best. Thirteen years then.

"We liked to take trips early on, early on in our marriage, and we had gone on some trips to Carolina Beach when we were first married and always had a good time. Your mama didn't always approve."

"Why?"

"Oh, we'd sit in bars now and then." She puts the Kleenex to one eye, then the other.

His mama could have told him this. It wasn't that bad.

"Then we stopped traveling so much and it seemed like in one way or another we were dealing with Tad's drinking, and I tried to get used to the fact that I was childless and would be, always. So then Margaret had you, and I started concentrating on being a good aunt, which I think I was."

"You certainly were—are." Carl pictures a kind of chart. The front nine-tenths of the chart shows Aunt Lil doing for him, and the final one-tenth, him doing for her.

Aunt Lil looks at her cigarette, takes a drag, taps it

over the sand. She dabs her eyes again with the Kleenex that by now has almost come apart. "His name was Bobby. When he showed up that day, Tad would have absolutely not one thing to do with him and asked him to leave. But before he did that—before Tad got home and asked him to leave—I got the story that the boy got from his real daddy's sisters.

"The couple that took him to Florida had gone to the orphanage looking for a baby, but they didn't have any. But the orphanage knew about Alice because she'd been by there, and they sent the Florida couple to her, and she gave him up, just gave him up, and so he'd had a hard life in Florida, working in orange groves, because this couple adopted kids to work in their groves for no pay, see— that was their plan.

"Now there Bobby was, come to see what his no-good stepfather looked like. And this was where I suddenly realized that if Tad hadn't sent him off, I'd at least have been able to raise a boy from the time he was five. I could have called him my own. At five years old is when I'd've got him. And he seemed to be such a nice young man, gentle." She was staring far away, shaking her head slowly.

Carl shifts his weight against the porch rail. "Do you know where he is now? Where he went?"

"Oh, no. What reason would he have to be anywhere close to here?" She looks back at Carl. "It's certainly not his home—this, around here, Hansen County."

"I guess not." For some reason, at that moment Carl sees Aunt Lil's apartment again—empty.

"When it settled on me what Tad had done, what he'd caused that boy to go through, what he'd denied me of, I tore up that marriage certificate and put it in the bottom of my trunk and then later in the file box, and in the last few years I've just . . . just wanted to remember the times at Carolina Beach, the good times, to forget all the bad, but I haven't been able to, so I thought if I got that marriage certificate glued back together somehow, that might help me put things back."

"I'll do it. I'll take care of that."

"I don't think it'll make any difference, really. And it was terrible taking care of him, Tad, when he finally got sick, just a nightmare, all the while me wondering about why I'd never done anything about it all. Just took it. And I always meant to tell him what I thought about what he'd done." She looks at Carl through her red eyes. "If there had just been some way to get back to the front of it."

"Front?"

"Back to right after we got married. I think that was my mistake in life: leaving myself out. Sometimes I . . . He was always good to you. I mean okay. Don't you think?"

"Uncle Tad? Oh, yeah. He was okay. I mean, he was always good to me. He never gave me any problem. But I never knew about all this other."

"Let's get back inside. It's kind of cool out here."

Part 4.

Come to Get My Aunt Out of Jail

Come to Get My Aunt Out of Jail

LIL CAN HARDLY BELIEVE what they've done, or where she *is*. In South Carolina. In jail. Thank goodness she has Carl's number written down, because she had forgotten it, and it's a wonder they didn't take her date book and everything else.

"Hello." He sounds sleepy.

"I'm in jail—in South Carolina."

"I don't think so, Aunt Lil. I think you're at Rose-haven."

"No, I'm not. They've got me in jail down here." He will believe her. If she just tells him two or three times, he will believe her.

"I'm in bed, Aunt Lil. I think you're at Rosehaven."

"I'm not either."

"Well, I'm sure of it. And . . . and let me tell you what I'm going to do. What I'm going to do is hang up the phone and then dial your Rosehaven number. And if it rings, that means you're at Rosehaven, that they've moved you back to Rosehaven."

"Do what?"

"When I tell you to, you hang up your phone. Then I'm going to call your number at Rosehaven. If your phone rings, that means they've brought you back."

"They haven't brought me anywhere except South Carolina. I'm in jail in South Carolina."

"Just hang up, and I'll call you right back, and you'll see where you are."

"I'm supposed to hang up the phone?"

"Yes ma'am. And then see if it rings. If it does, that means you're at Rosehaven, because that's the number I'm fixing to dial."

"Oh."

"Hang it up."

"Hang it up now?"

"Yes."

"Why? I just called." What is he talking about?

"Because we're going to do what I just said. I'm going to call your Rosehaven number so you can see if that's where you are."

"Okay." She hangs up. Why does he want to call her all the way down here in South Carolina before she explains anything?

Carl looks at the clock—a quarter past eleven. He presses the button, gets a dial tone, and dials her number.

"Hello?" she says.

"Hello, Aunt Lil? It's me. Carl."

"Carl, they've got me in a jail in South Carolina and you need to come get me out."

"No. You're at Rosehaven. See, I just called the Rosehaven number and you answered, so that means you're at Rosehaven."

"I'm in South Carolina—in jail. They've got the pictures and furniture just like it is at . . ."

"Rosehaven?"

"Yes. I know where I am, and I want you to come get me out, Carl. As soon as you can. They won't let me go unless you come."

"Okay, let me just do a couple of things, and I'll call you back or . . . come on down there."

"Okay. Good."

"Bye."

"Bye."

Carl calls the main desk. A Beverly answers. "Beverly, my aunt is Mrs. Olive in 309. She just called me, and she thinks she's locked up in a jail in South Carolina."

"I know. I was just down there. She won't go to bed—wouldn't come to supper either. I think she's just sundowning. She's not in any danger."

Not in any danger and doesn't know where the hell she is? thinks Carl. "Sundowning?"

"Yeah. Sometimes they get confused after the sun goes down."

"Okay. Tell her I'll be over there in a minute, if you don't mind. Just go down and let her know. And I think she might be in some danger inside her head, even if she's not on the outside, you know?"

"Sure, I'll get right on it."

CARL DRIVES TO ROSEHAVEN, parks his truck under the drive-under. The front door is locked, so he presses the intercom button and explains who he is. Beverly lets him in.

Aunt Lil is sitting in her big chair. Her little portable blackboard says, "Today is Wednesday, September 6, 2000." But it's Thursday night.

"Well, hey there," he says.

She swings her head and stares at him. "Who are you?"

"It's me. Carl."

She keeps staring. "Oh. Carl. Yes. I am so glad to see you." She reaches out a hand and he takes it.

He got here fast, she thinks. All that long way. He must have flown in an airplane. Why would these people do this to her? It's one of the strangest things that has ever happened. Nothing is going right anymore. The whole wide world is coming apart at the seams. But Carl stands right here now. Things are finally going to be okay.

Carl places his hand on her shoulder. She is skin and bones. What can be going on inside her head? He has a sudden idea. He kisses her on the cheek. "Let's go home."

"I am so glad. I don't know what I'd do without you. I am so glad you're here."

"Come on. Stand up. I'll hold your hand. We'll get you right back where you belong."

"I can make it." After a few tries, she stands up, takes hold of her walker. "Let me get my sweater. It was cold when I came in. It was like the halls of winter."

"I'll get it for you. Which one do you want? How about this blue one?"

"That's good. I'm certainly glad you're here. Is that the navy blue one?"

"Yes ma'am."

In the hall, Carl walks along very slowly so she can keep up.

She goes a little way and then stops and looks all around before starting out again. "They've made the place up to look just like Rosehaven. Look, they've got the very same pictures on the wall. Look at that. Look. I am so glad you're here."

"Yes ma'am."

It's late. Nobody is in the lobby except for Beverly, reading a magazine at the front desk.

At the truck, Carl folds her walker and places it in back. Her address book drops out. He puts it back. He helps her into the front seat, starts around the truck. Someone is coming up the driveway in a . . . wheelchair? It's L. Ray Flowers. What in the world is he . . . ?

L. Ray's hair is windblown. It's been washed, it looks like, but not sprayed. He's in his pajamas. "I've been for a little ride," he says. "Out one ear and in the other. That just came into my head."

There is something about the way L. Ray holds his head that seems off to Carl. Or is it his hair?

"I know the secret combination to the box on the side door," says L. Ray. "I like a night ride down the hill every once in a while. And this is my last week, so I decided to do it tonight."

"That hill?" Carl points to a side road that winds downhill in a wide curve.

"That's right. It takes longer to get back up. I go out about once every week or two. Is Miss Lil sick?"

"No." Carl checks the truck windows. They are up. "She thinks she's in South Carolina and I'm going to drive her back to Rosehaven."

"She's probably got a urinary tract infection. Or it's medicine. Open your door there so I can speak to her."

Carl opens the driver's door and L. Ray looks in. "Miss Lil? They got me down here too, and I'll be getting back to Rosehaven tomorrow. I'll meet you back there."

"Who is that?"

"L. Ray Flowers" says L. Ray, leaning in closer.

"I don't want him near me, Carl. He did that awful thing. You get away from me. Come on, Carl, let's go."

"Oh, mercy," says L. Ray as he backs away in his wheelchair. "I'm back where I damn well started. I . . . you all have a good trip."

"Thanks." Carl gets into the truck, closes his door. "What did he do?" he asks.

"Who?"

"L. Ray. Mr. Flowers."

"He started all this jail business. It has something to do with vulgarity, I think."

They take a right on Forrester, drive by Don's Pool and Dogs, which is closed—it's after midnight—on around the block, and then out to TechComm Commons and back around and into the driveway at Rosehaven.

"Well, here we are," says Carl.

"That was just an awful time. I don't know what I'd do without you."

"I'm glad I can help you out, Aunt Lil."

Beverly lets them in the front door.

Back in her room, she says, "You don't know. You don't know how it is. Nobody does. It's awful. Where's my gown?"

"Is this it?"

"Yes."

"I'll wait outside till you get dressed. Can I help?"

"No. I think I can do it. Sometimes I call them for

help, you know, but sometimes they don't come. I'm going to have to get somebody to help me out at night and in the morning. Do you think we can get Carrie?"

"We can sure try."

Carl waits in the hall while Aunt Lil gets dressed for bed. It takes a while. He looks in once, as she is getting her gown over her head, and sees her in only her underpants. He thinks of Holocaust photographs. He wanders down to the end of the hall, looks at a seascape painting for a while, then goes back, knocks on her door. Inside, he watches as she slowly manages to get under the covers.

"I'll see you soon," he says. "You be good."

Which one is he? Lil thinks.

LATER, JUST BEFORE she falls asleep, in the dim glow from the floodlight outside her window, she looks over at the photo of her business-school friends standing on those steps, waving. One by one, they grow larger, carefully stepping out of the photograph and into the room. She wants so badly to remember their names, but she can't. In her room, they make themselves at home, looking around, separating the blinds and looking out the window, helping themselves to Tootsie Rolls. Lil realizes that if she stays very still, they will not know she is there and she will not have to embarrass herself by speaking to them without remembering their names.

At the End of the Hall

CARL STOPS AT A red light, but no one is around and it's 3:00 A.M., so he runs it. It's Monday morning. After the jail episode, Aunt Lil had a fairly good weekend but felt bad on Sunday afternoon. Someone has just called from Rosehaven to tell him the rescue squad came to get her. She'd pulled the cord in her bathroom, and an aide found her unconscious. They could not find a DNR order and began CPR. When Carl arrives at the hospital, he has no idea what to expect. He's not clear about whether or not she has been revived. He's afraid a machine might be keeping her alive, something she said she didn't want; she signed a DNR order, he's sure, making that clear. Why can't they keep something like that straight? She *had* signed it, hadn't she?

A nurse at the emergency room desk sends him on back. The doctor on duty is Dr. James Starnes. "Come on in," he says. "She's right back here. I'm afraid there's not much hope. I'm sorry."

The doctor opens the big, wide door and Carl sees her. A nurse nods and leaves the room. Carl steps closer. The lights shine very bright. She is on her back with a thick pillow under her head so that she's positioned to look down across her feet, and a long tube—almost as big around as a flashlight—is in her mouth. Her tongue is hanging out beside the tube. Her eyelids are drooped over half-open eyes; they are perfectly still and dry, like a doll's eyes. Her sparse hair is out over her ears. Somehow she looks like a scarecrow, or a clown.

"She's not supposed to have that tube down her throat," says Carl. "She was supposed to be DNR."

"I'm bound by law until I get something in writing or verbally from the next of kin. You're the next of kin?"

"Yes. We had something on file at Rosehaven, I think."

"I'll turn this machine off. It's not helping her anyway. It's just a matter of time, with or without the breathing machine. Less than an hour, I'd say. I'm sorry."

The doctor walks over to the machine and stops it.

Carl rests his elbows on the bed railing, then places his hand on the cold hand resting on her stomach, and asks the doctor, "Is it okay if I try to close her eyes all the way?"

"By all means."

Carl closes her lids by pushing them down gently. They stay closed. He remembers something about coins on eyelids. He thinks about asking the doctor to remove the tube, but then decides not to. The machine is off. Pulling out that tube might disturb or hurt her in some awful way. Her gown is wide open at the neck—tight skin over bones, with the places at the base of her neck all hollowed out—and he sees a blue vein at her collarbone jump. He stares at it. "Is that her heart beating? That vein?"

"Yes. That's an artery." The doctor looks at a machine. "Her heart is beating only a few times a minute. That can't last very long."

Carl can't take his eyes away from the blue artery, the very slight, blue artery. He waits. It jumps. He starts counting slowly. At twenty it jumps again. Every twenty seconds —three times a minute. A pulse rate of three.

"I'll turn down the lights," says Dr. Starnes.

"Yes. Thank you."

Carl keeps his eye on the artery. It finally jumps again. He pushes her hair back behind one ear, then the other. The top of her head is almost completely bald. He follows an urge to rest his hand on her head. It feels like a cool, smooth cantaloupe, and then Dr. Starnes is standing across from him.

"So, she's your aunt?"

"My favorite aunt. She was like a second mother."

Carl notices that the artery hasn't jumped in a while. If it has, he missed it. Starnes is talking about something. Carl stares at the artery and starts counting. He counts to sixty while Starnes talks quietly.

Carl feels as if he might be up above the scene, watching.

"She's passed on now," says the doctor. "And sometimes people like to be alone with a loved one at this point. I'll be happy to wait outside."

"Yes, thanks."

"Out the door to the left, at the desk, is where I'll be," he says, "unless I'm occupied, in which case just leave me a note if you need to leave—there's a pencil and paper there. I think the form says Wayside Funeral Home. Is that right?"

"Yes. Thanks. I'll . . . I'll go get her wig and bring it back."

"That'll be fine. She'll be here for an hour or more, I'm sure." Starnes leaves, then sticks his head back in. "I should mention that it might be a good idea to go ahead and remove her wedding ring now."

"Okay. Sure."

Carl looks at her face again. The world is holding together, and Aunt Lil has just . . . died. He feels a tingling in his lips. The building and everything in the room is staying in its place. The light is steady, not changing. He picks up her hand. It is cold. "Aunt Lil, I'm sorry you had to go through all this. I thank you for all the attention you always gave me. Good-bye. . . . You're going to have to . . . to give up your driving."

He slides her ring over the second joint and then the first.

He is stunned, numb. Something comes up inside him that he instantly feels ashamed of: a stab of relief. He dismisses it.

There is a phone. He pulls out his billfold, gets Anna's business card, and dials all but the last digit of her home number, then hangs up.

He drives to Rosehaven. In Aunt Lil's room, he looks around—the La-Z-Boy, the Kennedy rocker, the footstool, her table, the bag of midget Tootsie Rolls. He removes her wig from the Styrofoam head, places his hand on that head in the same way he'd placed it on his aunt Lil's head in the emergency room. As he steps into the hall, he meets L. Ray Flowers, rolling his way. Carl looks at his watch. It's 4:35 A.M. L. Ray holds an envelope in his hand.

"I'm sorry about Miss Lil. I was awake and it didn't look good. How's she doing?"

"She died."

"I'm sorry. She was a mighty fine lady. Here. Here's a little note I was planning to leave for you. Read it when you get time. And you might as well wait until tomorrow night to try to sleep. Maybe a nap tomorrow afternoon. Voice of experience."

"Thanks. I will."

Dear Carl, my good man,

I think all the time, now. And this morning with your dear aunt en route to the hospital, I sit and think some more. And it's hard for me to avoid thinking as a preacher at a time like this.

Time is a very long hallway full of thick fog. All you see in front of you is whiteness. Far, far down that hallway, at the end of it, is a little campfire. It burns forever. But we don't see it, day to day. It marks the end of the hall, and you cannot see it because of all that fog.

We'll all be there quickly, as quickly as to-morrow's supper, and on approach to the camp-fire, somewhere in the bottom of our hearts there are tiny, sinking feelings of campfire knowl-edge. To prepare, we think of all the things we need to do before we get there, and one of your aunt Lil's gifts to the world, and to me, is her part in coming up with the idea of the First Breakfast. No matter if it happens or not.

In spite of the little campfire, we have all these good times and bad times, and then one day we happen to be looking out there in front of us and we see the glow, a faint little orange glow way down there ahead, at the end of the hallway, and it takes our breath for a minute, because we now see that in spite of it all, if we're lucky, we have loved every minute, no matter how good or bad, every minute that we've been in that white fog, and look at that . . . it's down there now: a very, very dull glow at the end of the hall.

Your aunt brought me hope toward the end of my hallway. And in my mind our little group will be there on the porch at Rosehaven, talking, until the stars fall and every porch and chair and church and nursing home in the world is reduced to a tiny, pure, young, and happy mote of dust that will be the cornerstone of yet another universe where there will be a First Breakfast Nurch in every town and village (there will be no cities) and we'll be playing the old hymns and other music every night of the week except Sunday evenings, when we'll all be at BTU (Baptist Training Union — remember?) studying the new word of the same old God. Huh?

Your good man, falsely accused,

L. Ray

As Carl, carrying the wig, enters the emergency room, he meets Anna coming out. They both stop. She reaches for him. He lets her hug him hard and is conscious of not hugging back as hard.

She stands back but holds to his arm. "I'm so sorry, Carl. They always call me. I couldn't get back to sleep, and so I was hoping I might catch you here. I just talked to Dr. Starnes. He told me."

"Yes . . . it's pretty hard." He holds out the wig. "I'm bringing this for her. She . . ." He knows he's about to cry, but he holds on hard. "I'm glad I was with her. Her vein, or artery, right here"—Carl touches his collarbone —"would jump once about every twenty seconds. And then it just stopped."

"We'll all miss her. But it's good she didn't have to suffer and linger for months."

"That's right. That's right. I'm not sure what I'll do now. Who's with your girls?" Shouldn't have asked that, he thinks.

Her face tells him.

Music Is Poetry Without Words

"SHE WAS A GOOD ONE," Carrie says. "She was spunky."

Carl sits on the porch after several trips to his truck to load Aunt Lil's belongings.

Little Maudie is here, in a wheelchair—she's fallen and sprained her knee—along with Clara, and a new woman, dressed in a red dress with a white scarf around her neck and wearing sunglasses. Maudie tells Carl how sorry she is about Lil, and then she asks Clara, "What is today, anyway?"

"I don't know. I don't care. I know it's a sad time— without Lil and Mr. Flowers."

"It's Saturday," says Carl. He checks his watch. Things seem empty.

"It is a sad time," says Maudie. "I miss Lil so much. But *he* had it coming. He was just too big for his britches, and the very idea that he did all that." Maudie turns to Carrie, frowning, a touch of panic in her eyes. "Do you know if my niece will be here today?"

"I don't know for sure. Today is Saturday, though, so she'll probably be here in a little while."

"Will you roll me in?" Maudie says to the new lady.

"I'll roll you in," says Carrie.

"No. I want her to roll me in."

"I can't do that right now," says the new lady.

"Will you roll me in?" Maudie asks Carl. She looks worried.

"Sure. I need to be getting on, too."

They roll along the hall. Maudie's door is open — 307, next to Aunt Lil's room. Carl glances in. He doesn't know the aide changing the bed.

"Just push me over beside that table, where I can watch the television. . . . There we go. That's good. Thank you very much." A basketball game is on the TV.

The room smells like carpet cleaner. Carl hears a vacuum cleaner come on in the next room. Wouldn't be a Kirby. What will he do with that Kirby? Should he have buried it with her? They would have in Egypt.

"Would you like some candy?" asks Maudie.

"I don't think so."

"It's those candy Kisses. Can you get me the bag out of that drawer right there? Right there."

"Certainly."

"I don't see why you don't have one. Or two. It's hard to eat just one. Oh, look, the basketball game is on. Carolina's playing. Don't you want to pull up a chair and watch a little of the game?"

"I—"

"Look at that. The other team scored. Carolina wears the Carolina blue. Those boys are so tall. Look at that little bitty referee. Have another Kiss."

"Thank you." He continues to stand. The candy aisle at Eckerd flashes into his mind. How many times in the last months had he been unable to find the midget Tootsie Rolls, but kept looking and finally found them?

"They got rid of that preacher. I guess you know that."

"Yes, I heard."

"I'm afraid somebody else will get in here and start doing the same things. Have another Kiss."

"Okay. One more. Then I've got to be getting on."

"You've got to go to work?"

"Yes ma'am, and maybe stop in somewhere to get a bite to eat first."

"I used to work in a lawyer's office. Boy, that was something."

"I'll bet it was."

They watch the ball game for a minute or two.

"I've got to be getting along now," Carl says. "You take it easy."

"I will. You too. Will you do something for me?"

He wants out of there. "What's that?"

"Will you turn up the volume? I never can figure out that flashlight thing with all the buttons—what do you call it?"

"Remote."

"That's right."

On the porch, Carrie listens as the new woman says, "My niece's son just got a dozen crows tattooed on his butt like they're flying out his butt hole, and her not having a man around the house to keep those kids straight is about to drive her crazy."

"How did you find that out?" says Mrs. Cochran.

"He's been gone four years—it'd drive anybody crazy, with a teenage boy and a nine-year-old girl."

"No, how do you know about the crows?"

"Her daughter told me. She tells me everything. Sweetest thing."

"Why would somebody want a tattoo of crows flying out their ass?" asks Mrs. Cochran.

"I don't know. Why would anybody want a tattoo of anything flying out their ass?"

Oh, that's good, thinks Carrie. We've got another one of those.

"It's okay to have a tattoo to show you're in the army," says Mrs. Cochran. "That's what they used to do. But my Lord, did he have six crows on each cheek or what?"

"Beats the hell out of me."

Silence. A few people leave and a few arrive.

The new woman continues, "Do you want me to find out?"

"No, I just wondered."

"My daughter used to get all over me for bringing home food from the Golden Corral. I told her they didn't care and she said it was stealing, and I told her it won't because I paid. Me and my friend Agatha Marrs used to go in there at about ten-thirty, and that way we got in on the breakfast and the lunch. Catch them during the changeover. We ate all we could hold, and I'd end up with a piece of chicken, a piece of ham, and a piece of sausage in my pocketbook, wrapped up in napkins. Why don't we go and do that one day?"

"I'm not up to going out much anymore. And we've lost our driver."

"One day I thought I had a muffin, but it must have got lost somewhere. I looked for it in the car and couldn't find it. I used plastic bags in case something leaked. After we left there, we'd go to Sears and then Kroger's and then Byrd's and then Harris Teeter. A lot of times they had plants on sale at Harris Teeter. And Agatha was always buying plants. She also made beautiful rugs — from rags. A full day, it was, that she and I would have, and I wish you could have been with us. We had so much fun. We could go about anywhere we wanted to. We just took a notion one time and drove to the mountains. Saw some Cherokee Indians. Those were the days."

Carrie watches Carl walk across the porch and raise a hand. "See you all later," he says. Carrie thinks about Mrs. Olive, his aunt.

"Bye, son," says Mrs. Cochran. "There goes Carl," she says to the new woman. "He was so good to Lil. She's the one who just passed away."

"What does he do for a living?"

"Makes awnings. I hate to see him go. He's a good sport. A good singer too. I liked to hear him sing. I liked to hear Mr. Flowers too. I wish he was still here. He got a raw deal. But he says he's coming back to see us. He's starting a world movement, and some of us helped him get it going."

"I like music," says the new woman.

"Music is poetry without words," says Mrs. Cochran. "I had a teacher who used to say that."

"I never read much poetry that I could understand."

"I don't think you're supposed to understand it. You're supposed to feel it—like music."

"Or like a window fan."

"That's not what I meant," says Mrs. Cochran, "but I see what you mean."

At her supper table, Faye Council, the physical therapist, says to her husband, Manley, "We lost another two this week. One died, and the other got run out. I liked them both."

"Why?"

"I just did. They were both sort of—"

"No—why did one get run out?"

"He was involved in some kind of under-the-covers stuff. I never got the straight of it. He's that preacher I told you about. The one with the crazy sermons. He was preaching and playing music with Mrs. Olive's nephew in the activity room one or two nights a week."

"Pass that, please."

"I don't think Mr. Rhodes liked him."

"He's the one that runs the hardware, right? Or is that his daddy?"

"He runs lots of places. I think his daddy is retired."

Rank Strangers

IT'S EARLY SPRING, and Carl stands at the sink in L. Ray's kitchen, stripping collard leaves from stems.

L. Ray sits at the kitchen table, a walker beside his chair. He brings a cigar to his mouth with his left hand, inhales. A stroke has left him partially paralyzed, and home health care ran out yesterday. No more speech therapy, occupational therapy, physical therapy. "I'm glad that's over," he says. "That is some useless, 'pensive stuff."

"At least you didn't have to pay for it—most of it."

"Are you pulling off the leaves top-down?"

"I hadn't thought about it."

"It's lots easier top-down."

Gladys, L. Ray's niece, left two hours earlier, headed

back to Topsail Island. "This is really it," she said to Carl out on the porch. "I'm sorry he can't stay here, and I'm sorry you got just one bedroom, but I've done all I can, more times than I should have, and I've got my own family to look after. Just get him in that place for me, and then I'll be back first chanst I get."

L. Ray is scheduled to arrive at Pine Valley Grove by 3:00 P.M. The name was changed from Shady Rest the weekend before—as a consequence of some incidents, a big fine, and bad publicity.

"Why do you need to cook them separate?" asks Carl.

"The stems take longer. Lot of people th-throw the sta-stems away, but if you cut them up f-fine an' cook them longer 'n the leaves, then it's add flavor."

"Have you got a knife sharpener?"

"There's a . . . witstone . . . whetstone in the drawer beside . . . yes, that one."

"I think my mama just put them in all together, but I don't know what she seasoned them with."

"Vinegar, s-sugar, and that can of . . ."

"Chicken broth. And all you want is black-eyed peas and corn bread to go with them?"

"Right. Gladys got that out. Right there. If you want some meat, there's some bacon, I think. You can take what's er-ver in there. God, I hate to go that place."

"I hate to take you."

"Maybe they'll kick me outen his . . . his . . . this one too."

"What is the real reason you had to leave Rosehaven?" Carl stops stripping leaves from the collards. "Did you really, you know, do what they said, in front of that woman?"

"Masturbage . . . -bate?"

"Yes."

"You think I would thing a . . . do a thing like that? Who would do a thing like that?"

"I'm asking you."

"Of course not. Of course not. I knew her one time, it turns out, but God knows that was a century ago. What you say they call this language thing again?"

"Aphasia."

"That's right. You know, whoever wrote up all that speech and therapy stuff is silly."

LATE THE NEXT AFTERNOON, a warm early-spring day, L. Ray and Carl sit in plastic chairs under a tree in the yard at Pine Valley Grove. A walker sits beside L. Ray's chair. A guitar lies in a case between them. There is no porch. L. Ray brings a cigar to his mouth with his left hand, inhales. Carl is peeling an orange.

Most of the other residents are eating dinner.

Carl has brought along a CD player and a copy of the new CD of his and L. Ray's songs recorded by the Mac Faircloth Band. After they hear the last song, L. Ray says, "That worked out fine."

"Yeah, it did, didn't it? I appreciate you getting me going on it."

"I'm much obliged for . . . for everything."

They sit for a while.

"A hundred thousand . . . jears . . . years ago," says L. Ray, "we lef' old people under a tree, or et . . . ate them so we could go on and . . . and take care of the chi'ren, and hunt, and plant cr- . . . cr- . . ."

"Crops."

"Maybe we should go brack . . . back to that."

"That's a little far-fetched, don't you think?"

"Of course, but it makes a point. When will the TVM . . . TV people start wha'ever they're going do? When they begin?"

"I don't think they will."

"Well, I do."

"They won't. They won't be here."

"I'm the one who talk to them, and besides 'at, who ask you?"

"You did."

Somehow Carl is going to have to tell L. Ray that they are without disciples. No rush on that, though.

They sit in silence.

"Let's play 'Rank Strangers,'" says Carl. He picks up the guitar. "You sing it."

"Rank Strangers" has long stretches of nothing but music between sung phrases, and during these times, Carl feeds L. Ray the words of next line.

Epilogue

Songs by Carl Turnage
and L. Ray Flowers

AIN'T GOT NO PROBLEMS
by Turnage and Flowers

I got throwed in jail last summer,
Beat up by a jailhouse mob.
Got let out in September,
Went out and found a job.
My girlfriend has not left me,
My truck is not broke down,
My hair is thick and curly,
And my lost dog is found.

Chorus:
Ain't got no problems,
And that's my problem.
Lord, help me find something wrong.

My boss man was a screamer,
Unnecessarily.
Then I got promoted,
And now he works for me.
My rent has been reduced one-third.
I sleep like a baby at night.
My clothes now all fit me,
And my dentures are tight.

Chorus:
Ain't got no problems,
And that's my problem.
Lord, help me find something wrong.

I quit all my drinking,
Quit all my fighting.
Got me a new career called
Country-song writing.
All I wanted to do today
Is write one country song,
But how can I do that
When nothing is wrong?

Chorus:
Ain't got no problems,
And that's my problem.
Lord, help me find something wrong
So I can write a country song.

THE SAFETY PATROL SONG
        by Turnage and Flowers

Chorus:
I'd like to be on the safety patrol,
Wear a clean white strap,
Shine my shoes and stand up straight,
And wear a sailor's cap.

I saw Joe at recess.
He told me about his plan
To drop a cherry bomb down the boys' commode.
He wants to be a dynamite man.
But I can't be a dynamite man
Because, as I've been told,
If you drop a cherry bomb down the boys' commode
You can't be on the safety patrol.

Chorus:
I'd like to be on the safety patrol,
Wear a clean white strap,
Shine my shoes and stand up straight,
And wear a sailor's cap.

I saw Floyd after football practice.
He was sipping on a glass of brew.
He said, "Pull up a chair and have a drink, old friend.
Here's to me and you."
But I can't drink with all my friends
Because, as I've been told,
If you touch one drop of alcohol
You can't be on the safety patrol.

Epilogue

Chorus:
I'd like to be on the safety patrol,
Wear a clean white strap,
Shine my shoes and stand up straight,
And wear a sailor's cap.

I saw Faye in 4-H Club.
She handed me a letter.
It said, "Meet me down behind the gym.
I'd like to get to know you better."
But I can't go down behind the gym
Because, as I've been told,
If you fornicate or matriculate
You can't be on the safety patrol.

Chorus (much slower):
Who gives a dern for the safety patrol.
I think I've changed my mind.
I'll be down behind the gym,
Having a good old time.

BALONEY, BACON, AND BEER
   by Turnage and Flowers

All I wanted was pork and beans—
A can or two or more.
But where she does her shopping
Is a fancy health-food store
Where all the fruit's organic
And chickens run on the range.
I packed my bags and left;
I needed an organic change.

Chorus:
Baloney, bacon, and beer
Works morning, noon, and night.
Throw in a jar of ballpark mustard
And a loaf of bread that's white.
What the hell's halibut?
And who can eat soup that's cold?
A grocery store without pork and beans
Is a store without a soul.

I've been gone six weeks now.
I feel like I'm doing fine.
I've done without cilantro,
Done without French wine.
I've saved a good deal of money.
Don't listen to NPR.
I keep my food in a cooler
'Cause I live in my car.

Epilogue

Chorus:
Baloney, bacon, and beer
Works morning, noon, and night.
Throw in a jar of ballpark mustard
And a loaf of bread that's white.
What the hell's halibut?
And who can eat soup that's cold?
A grocery store without pork and beans
Is a store without a soul.

They say what you eat is what you are
And what you can't, you ain't.
I'll tell you one thing:
I never feel faint.
I've got me a new situation
And all the rules are clear.
I got my own refrigerator—
Stocked with baloney, bacon, and beer.

Chorus:
Baloney, bacon, and beer
Works morning, noon, and night.
Throw in a jar of ballpark mustard
And a loaf of bread that's white.
What the hell's halibut?
And who can eat soup that's cold?
A grocery store without pork and beans
Is a store without a soul.
A grocery store without iceberg lettuce
Is a store without a soul.

How Come I Miss You When You're with Me All the Time?
by Turnage and Flowers

We stay together constantly.
We never fight; we just agree.
If I go for a walk, you're right behind.
How come I miss you when you're with me all the time?

I know I have grown bigger since we met.
Sometimes I look around and I forget
That we're in love and doing fine.
How come I miss you when you're with me all the time?

Chorus:
How come I miss you when you're with me all the time?
Could it be my one-track mind?
Or is it that our love has stalled
Because I've grown so big and you're so small?

You warned me once and then again
If I ate too much, our love could end.
You're clearly not the straying kind.
How come I miss you when you're with me all the time?

And now I'm so big, all I can see
Is nothing in the world . . . but me.
Speak up, little darlin'; I don't mind.
How come I miss you when you're with me all the time?

Chorus:
How come I miss you when you're with me all the time?
Could it be my one-track mind?

Epilogue

Or is it that our love has stalled
Because I've grown so big and you're so small?
Because I've grown so big and you're so small.

FAT FROM SHAME
   by Turnage and Flowers

When I was just a child
We never left no food behind.
We never left none on the table.
We'd been the wasteful kind.

My mama, she was overweight;
My daddy, he was too.
And if a bare bone was left,
We fed it to Old Blue.

Chorus:
I'm fat from shame—
My mama is to blame.
We ate everything on the table.
Fat from shame—
My mama is to blame.
I eat every biscuit I'm able.

We ate what was before us
And never saved a cent.
Bought fatback from the grocery store,
Could hardly pay the rent.

My mama, she stayed overweight,
But Old Blue, he died one night.
I figured we'd eat him too,
Just so we'd do what's right.
Chorus:
I'm fat from shame—
My mama is to blame.
We ate everything on the table.

Epilogue

Fat from shame—
My mama is to blame.
I eat every biscuit I'm able.

Now we have three children
And they all have beer guts.
We built a little brewery.
We drive the neighbors nuts.

We sit around the table.
We don't stand a lot.
And one thing you can bet on:
Skinny we're not.

Chorus:
I'm fat from shame—
My children are to blame.
They eat everything on the table.
Fat from shame—
My children are to blame.
I eat every biscuit,
all the corn bread,
all the chicken,
all the dumplings,
all the taters,
all the gravy,
all the pork chops
I'm able.

LUNCH AT THE PICCADILLY

A Reader's Guide

CLYDE EDGERTON

A CONVERSATION WITH
CLYDE EDGERTON

Q: Many writers would balk at the idea of writing about a nursing home. Why did you decide it was a worthy setting for a novel and, given the topics of many bestsellers, was this risky?

A: Nursing homes house extreme loneliness and pain (think about how much better our culture cares for some old Thoroughbreds than some old people) but also humor and heroism—from clients, workers, and caretakers. While some low-paid aides are lax, some are saints. Sometimes clients' families, especially middle-aged and older children, suffer from despair but are reluctant to talk about that despair. That's probably a consequence of guilt, some justified, some not. I didn't feel the subject was risky. My parents were relatively old when I was born, I was an only child, and I had over twenty aunts and uncles, many of whom were like grandparents to me. They all made me feel secure, and I felt at home with them. I learned that their stories tended to have a kind of final—and thus more poignant—drama than the drama of many young people's stories. So, rather than risky, it seemed like a worthy subject.

Q: Were there any specific incidents that got you started on the book?

A: In 1996 my aunt was in a nursing home and I was writing at the time, didn't have a "day job," so I could visit her at eleven in the morning or three in the afternoon. One afternoon I was cutting her toenails. She looked over at her roommate Ernestine and said, "Don't you wish you had a nephew who'd come in and do for you like this one does for me?" Ernestine said, "I got two nephews. They both work." I knew a scene like that belonged in a book.

Q: Was it a difficult book to write?

A: Yes. I had to write many drafts because I was too close to it. I don't have good perspective as a writer when I'm too close to my story. I need distance because distance gives me perspective and that brings some objectivity and then I can write. When you're coming out of a relationship you are often still too close to it to write about it. You don't have the distance you need. There are several ways to get the distance you need to write about a situation: You can move to another country or another state; you can take notes and wait a long time; you can write through it. This one I wrote through and that was difficult.

Q: Are the characters in the novel based on anyone in particular?

A: They're pretty much composites. In my mind I have a wall with a window in it, and there are real people on one side and imaginary people on the other. Sometimes I reach through the window from the fiction side and get characteristics to give to the people in my stories. So the characters I end up with in my stories sometimes resemble people I know in the way cousins or neighbors may resemble one another. But I never feel like I'm writing about real people, and readers who assume so are wrong.

Q: What do you hope the reader will take away from *Lunch at the Piccadilly*?

A: Certainly a pleasurable experience. I try to avoid consciously writing about messages, although it's fun to watch L. Ray Flowers preach his messages. But I do distinguish his messages from mine. I think the idea of Nurch is a good idea and it's fun to let him run with it. I don't like to be openly and harshly critical of organized religion and I don't like to hear anyone else do it, because organized religion is too complicated to bash in general. I grew up in a Southern Baptist church where the adults were like aunts and uncles to me. I felt totally safe and secure in that environment. Though, on the other hand, I do believe that some fundamentalists would like a state-based fundamentalist religion where people who sinned would be punished. I'm glad America was founded in part to keep things such as that from happening.

I'd also like the reader to come away with an awareness of the responsibilities of the caretaker. No one is ever prepared for that responsibility and there is so much guilt involved. It's one of those things you don't want to prepare for. Like being in the army. You don't want to prepare to be in the army. You get in the army and it's so bad that when it's over you don't want to talk about it because it was so awful. Usually the caretaker is a son or a daughter and usually they are so ashamed of their negative feelings about it, they don't talk about it. That's a very traumatic time for many people, and when it's over you don't talk about it because it's over. So I hope that perhaps those who haven't experienced it might use this book as a starting place for conversations.

Q: How was your experience in taking care of an aunt and your mother similar or dissimilar to Carl's?

A: My experience was similar to Carl's in that I kept visualizing my aunt's apartment (that I associated with her) as empty and my sitting on the floor with my back against the wall. This was easier to visualize than visualizing me without her. My experience is different than Carl's because I had a different job than he did, was married with children, and was a good bit older. But I used some of my own emotions in describing his.

Q: Can you tell us about your inspiration for the character L. Ray Flowers and perhaps a little background on some of his "prayers" and "sermons"?

A: The inspiration came from any number of evangelists I have read about or known. In early drafts of the novel the convalescent center had a voice of its own and some of those voices were made into sermons. I wanted L. Ray to be very lively and different from most evangelists. He was retired, after all, and also didn't have a specific congregation that he was bound to keep happy. So he was free to preach whatever was on his mind. I allowed myself to be very creative with his prayers and sermons, and I hope readers realize that characters in fiction are supposed to be like characters in real life—that is, they can think and say anything imaginable and what they think may or may not be what the author thinks.

Q: How did you do research for this novel?

A: My experience as caretaker for two aunts and my mother over a span of eleven years or so was my research in the main, although I hasten that much of my caretaking was enjoyable and not as stressful as what many people experience. I also had more help than some people have. A cousin of mine, Ola King, lived with my mother for the last two years of her life, cooked for her, and took care of her during serious illnesses. I was lucky to have her.

It was important for me not to make fun of old people who are victims in my novel. So I edited carefully for passages that might come across that way, and the four elderly women who are the main characters in the novel are anything but victims. Like my mother and aunts—they enjoyed seeing the funny side of life, and they enjoyed talking and telling stories.

Q: Do you have any specific concerns about getting old?

A: A good friend, Lex Matthews, once told me that there are four stages of life: spring, summer, fall, and winter. He said the ability to live each stage well (for example, with laughter and grace) depended very much on how the stage before it was lived. And I think he was right about that. I think having a few good friends at any stage in life is important for mental health—very important. And one of the saddest things about getting into the winter stage of life is that we begin losing some of our best friends.

Q: What do you hope readers get from your novel?

A: I hope that readers with aging parents get a little notion of what is likely to come in their lives, and I hope those

experiencing hardships realize that they are not alone—
that others are having similar experiences. I would hope
that they seek help when they feel tired and hopeless—
whether the help is from a preacher, counselor, friend,
or one of many groups of people who meet to talk about
aging issues. I hope they will realize that it is okay to be angry and to feel guilty and to be upset about their predicament, that this is human, and that talking about their
feelings is okay and often a good thing.

Q: How do you feel about novels that are written to con-
vey messages?

A: Messages are for preachers and essayists. Stories are for
novelists. Sometimes stories have messages, intended or
not. Some people are born to be preachers. They should
preach. Some are born to write essays and that's what they
should do. My bent is telling stories, and I hope to not con-
fuse that role with the first two, because we all offer something different and, likewise, I think people like to listen to
sermons of one sort or another, to read essays about life,
and also to read made-up stories about made-up people,
because all three can be sources of humor, insight, and
pleasure. Writing *Lunch at the Piccadilly* was one way that
I took the experience of caretaker in my own life and made
something new out of it, something that I hope will come
alive for readers—at least long enough for them to forget
their troubles and remember gifts they've received over the

years from friends and family. And perhaps remind them of the humor in their own lives. But I try to avoid thinking about passing on specific messages as I write stories, because that can get in the way of the story, and the book then ends up with characters who mouth the beliefs of the writer.

Reading Group Questions and Topics for Discussion

1. Compare the relationship of Carl and Lil with similar relationships you know about or have experienced.

2. How does the dementia of characters in this novel compare with actual cases you know about?

3. Did the episode about Lil's marriage certificate add to or detract from the novel's plot? Why?

4. Would you rate the moral life of L. Ray Flowers "good," "bad," or somewhere in between? Why?

5. Does the "back story" about Darla and L. Ray detract from or add to the novel?

6. Describe differences you have observed among residences for the elderly. Why do you believe these differences exist?

7. Where have you confronted situations and language such as that found in the prologue to *Lunch at the Piccadilly*?

8. Does the music written by Carl and L. Ray add to or distract from the plot of the novel? Why?

9. Do you detect any changes in Carl during the story? If so, elaborate.

10. How do you feel about the use of humor in a story about the elderly?

11. In two short sentences, say what you believe this novel is about.

12. Would you describe the ending of this novel as upbeat? a downer? something else? Why?

CLYDE EDGERTON is the author of seven bestsellers, including *Raney, Walking Across Egypt,* and *Where Trouble Sleeps.* Five of his novels have been *New York Times* Notable Books. A musician and songwriter, he lives with his wife and their young son in Wilmington, North Carolina, where he is a professor of creative writing at the University of North Carolina at Wilmington.